They stayed like that for more than a minute.

Then his head lifted slightly and his eyelashes brushed against her forehead before he dropped a gentle kiss on her head. His other hand came up and rested at the back of her hair. 'Thank you for coming with me today, Samantha.'

The words were stuck in her throat. Anything that came out right now would make her sound like a blundering idiot. This was crazy, but it felt special. She didn't feel like a teenage fan girl any more. She certainly didn't feel like his nurse. She felt something else entirely.

She stared down at their still intertwined hands. It was so much easier than looking up—if she did they'd be nose to nose, and she didn't even want to guess as to what might happen next.

She sucked in a breath to steady her nerves and licked her oh-so-dry lips. 'Any time, Mitchell.'

Dear Reader

Christmas is one of my favourite times of year. My last two Christmas books have been based in my nearest city, Glasgow. This year I decided to go to another Christmas setting—Innsbruck in Austria.

My nurse, Samantha Lewis, is desperate—she needs to work as an agency nurse to pay her mother's nursing home fees. She's used to dealing with children, but her assignment this year is a little unusual: help Mitchell Brody come to terms with being newly diagnosed with diabetes.

Problem 1: Mitchell Brody is an adult.

Problem 2: Mitchell Brody is a rock star—think Michael Hutchence from INXS.

Problem 3: Mitchell Brody has no intention of being 'managed' by anyone.

Problem 4: Being in a house with a gorgeous rock star is more than a little distracting…

Here's to the season of goodwill! I hope you enjoy Sam and Mitchell's story. Please feel free to tell me what you think at www.scarlet-wilson.com. I love to hear from readers!

Scarlet Wilson

CHRISTMAS WITH THE MAVERICK MILLIONAIRE

BY
SCARLET WILSON

MILLS & BOON

First published in Great Britain 2014
by Mills & Boon, an imprint of Harlequin (UK) Limited,
Eton House, 18-24 Paradise Road, Richmond, Surrey, TW9 1SR

© 2014 Scarlet Wilson

ISBN: 978-0-263-24339-0

Printed and bound in Great Britain
by CPI Antony Rowe, Chippenham, Wiltshire

Scarlet Wilson wrote her first story aged eight and has never stopped. Her family have fond memories of *Shirley and the Magic Purse*, with its army of mice, all with names beginning with the letter 'M'. An avid reader, Scarlet started with every Enid Blyton book, moved on to the *Chalet School* series and many years later found Mills & Boon®.

She trained and worked as a nurse and health visitor, and currently works in public health. For her, finding Mills & Boon® Medical Romance™ was a match made in heaven. She is delighted to find herself among the authors she has read for many years.

Scarlet lives on the West Coast of Scotland with her fiancé and their two sons.

Recent titles by Scarlet Wilson:

TEMPTED BY HER BOSS
A MOTHER'S SECRET
200 HARLEY STREET: GIRL FROM THE RED CARPET†
HER FIREFIGHTER UNDER THE MISTLETOE
ABOUT THAT NIGHT…**
THE MAVERICK DOCTOR AND MISS PRIM**
AN INESCAPABLE TEMPTATION
HER CHRISTMAS EVE DIAMOND
A BOND BETWEEN STRANGERS*
WEST WING TO MATERNITY WING!
THE BOY WHO MADE THEM LOVE AGAIN
IT STARTED WITH A PREGNANCY

†*200 Harley Street*
*The Most Precious Bundle of All
**Rebels with a Cause

Dedication

This book is dedicated to my fellow 'mums',
Fiona Bell, Hazel Inch, Wendy Imrie,
Deanne McLachlan, Fiona Kennedy, Karen Wallace
and, in pastures new, Jeanette Aitken.

Our children are fast on the way to adulthood and
it's getting pretty scary. It's great to have friends to
share this with. Christmas nights out are never dull!

Praise for
Scarlet Wilson:

'HER CHRISTMAS EVE DIAMOND is a fun and
interesting read. If you like a sweet romance with just
a touch of the holiday season you'll like this one.'
—*harlequinjunkie.com*

'WEST WING TO MATERNITY WING! is a tender,
poignant and highly affecting romance that is sure
to bring a tear to your eye. With her gift for creating
wonderful characters, her ability to handle delicately
and compassionately sensitive issues and her talent
for writing believable, emotional and spellbinding
romance, the talented Scarlet Wilson continues to
prove to be a force to be reckoned with in the world
of contemporary romantic fiction!'
—*cataromance.com*

CHAPTER ONE

SAMANTHA LEWIS RAN UP the steps of the agency, pulling her bright pink scarf from her head and scattering a trail of raindrops behind her. The forecast had been clear, but she should have known better in damp London in the middle of December.

As she pushed open the door she was hit by a wave of heat and a rush of noise. No one in the agency seemed to sit down. It was constantly busy, dealing with desperate calls for specialised nursing care over the holiday season. She undid the buttons on her thick grey duffel and tried to find somewhere to perch until she could speak to someone.

It shouldn't be long. She already knew where her assignment would be, and who she'd be looking after—she just needed confirmation. Looking after Daniel Banks—a seven-year-old with cystic fibrosis—was really the perfect job for her. Three weeks' work for the equivalent of six months' worth of her current NHS salary. A match made in heaven.

It was hard work, but Daniel was a gorgeous little boy who needed round-the-clock care. His family clearly adored him, and having an extra pair of hands—expert hands—to watch their little boy over the Christmas period benefited them all.

She caught the eye of Leah, the receptionist, and gave

her a smile. But Leah, who was normally so friendly, looked away quickly and picked up the phone again. Strange.

She watched for a few minutes as a couple of familiar faces appeared, picked up their assignments and headed off back out into the throng of Oxford Street. At least she wasn't alone. Most other nurses she knew wanted to spend time with their families at Christmas.

Then there were the few who were just as desperate as she was. This was the best-paying gig of the year. The last two years she'd lucked out with Daniel's fantastic family. Some of her other colleagues hadn't been so fortunate and had spent the festive period being a cross between a house-maid, a nanny and, in one case, a cook, as well as a nurse.

There was a stiff breeze at her side as another door opened. Trish, the owner, stuck her head out. 'Sam, in here, please.'

She started fastening the buttons on her duffel again. Even though they were inside, the wind whipping around Trish's office was worse than the current gale blowing down Oxford Street. Trish Green was going through the 'change' and her staff knew all about her flushes and had warned everyone not to mention a thing.

'What's up, Trish? Aren't you just going to give me my assignment?'

She closed the office door behind her as Trish gestured to the seat in front of her desk. She couldn't help but notice the troubled look on Trish's face. The happy, shining feeling she'd had while climbing the stairs was starting to leave her.

Trish's face was flushed red as she sat down at the other side, a file clasped in her hand. 'I'm sorry, Sam. I did try to call you.' She hesitated for a second, as if she knew the impact of what she was about to say. 'Daniel Banks was hospitalised last night.'

Sam sat straight up. 'Is he okay? What's wrong with him? Is it a chest infection?'

Chest infections were pretty common for kids with CF and Sam was a specialist, she could give IV antibiotics and extensive physio if required. Trish licked her lips and took a deep breath as she shook her head. 'Nothing so simple. It's pneumonia. He's been ventilated.'

Tears sprang to the corners of her eyes. This was serious. Pneumonia could be deadly to a kid like Daniel. 'No! How is he doing? Have you spoken to his parents? Is there anything we can do?'

Trish sighed. 'Yes, I've spoken to them. They've been warned that all plans will need to be cancelled. They're in it for the long haul.'

Sam rested back in the wobbly chair. Daniel was a lovely little boy, so full of joy, so full of fun, with a body that betrayed his spirit. She couldn't imagine how the family must be feeling.

'Sam?' She looked up.

Trish had worry lines along her brow like deep furrows in the ground. 'I'm sorry, but it means your assignment will be cancelled.'

A chill swept over her body, every tiny little hair standing on end as her breath caught in her chest. It hadn't even entered her brain. Of course, she couldn't work for Daniel's family now. And, of course, she wouldn't be paid.

It was a horrible set of circumstances. Trouble was, her mother's nursing-home fees would still need to be paid at the end of the month. This was why she was here. This was the reason she gave up her holidays every year.

Her chest tightened. She still hadn't released the breath she was holding. She was trying not to let panic consume her. Trying not to say all the words out loud that were currently circulating like a cyclone in her brain. How on earth was she going to pay the fees?

Trish shifted uncomfortably in her chair. 'I had a quick look before you got here, Sam. I don't really have anything similar. I certainly don't have anything that lasts for three weeks and pays the same fee.' She shuffled some papers on her desk. 'I've got a patient requiring terminal care but they're in Ireland, a woman with dementia who needs to be accompanied on a flight to Barbados, and a child with an infectious disease who basically needs to be babysat while the rest of the family go on their Christmas cruise.'

'They're going on holiday without their kid?' She couldn't hide the disgust in her voice. 'What happened to holiday medical insurance and cancelling for another date?'

Trish couldn't look her in the eye. 'The father can't get other holidays, so the rest of the family have to go without the child.'

'That's shocking. Who does something like that?'

Trish shoved the paper under the others on her desk. 'Didn't think that one would be for you.'

The door opened and Leah hesitated in the doorway. 'Eh, Trish? That query earlier—it just came in. It's a definite. Flight's at seven from Gatwick. We need someone now.'

Trish's eyes flickered from side to side, between Leah and Samantha. She bit her lip and took the file from Leah's hand, opening it and sitting it on her desk. For a few moments she scanned the page in front of her.

Sam couldn't stand the silence—it let her hear the thoughts currently circulating in her head. 'Anything I can do?' Was that her voice, sounding so desperate? Had she really just said that out loud?

She needed a job. She needed something that paid her for the next three weeks, otherwise she'd need to go back and plead for extra bank shifts. Would three weeks' overtime pay in the NHS equal what she would get at the agency? Not even close.

Trish fixed her steely gaze on her. She cleared her throat. 'How are you with diabetes, Samantha?'

Sam straightened in the chair. It wasn't easy as every

time she moved, the wobbly legs threatened to throw her to the floor. She couldn't help but search her brain desperately. 'I'm fine. I mean, I'm good. No, I'm better than good.'

Yip. Definitely sounding desperate.

Trish's eyebrows had risen, a look of pure disbelief on her face. If this was the difference between getting another job or not, it was time to put on the performance of a lifetime.

Sam took a deep breath. 'Obviously, I know all the basics as a nurse. But my sister is diabetic, diagnosed as a child. I know about hypos, high blood sugars, adjusting insulin doses and all the risks and complications.' It was true. She did know more than the average nurse. Living with someone with diabetes as a child was a whole different ballgame from looking after a patient for a few days in a hospital.

Trish was still studying her carefully. 'How do you feel about working with someone who's just been diagnosed? You'd have to do the entire education package and training with them.'

Sam licked her lips and nodded slowly. The fundamentals of diabetes hadn't changed over the years. She'd watched her sister change monitoring systems and insulin regimes many times. The most important factor was always going to be steady blood-sugar levels. 'I think I can manage that without any problems. What age is the patient?'

Trish was still shuffling papers on her desk. 'Do you have a current passport? And how do you feel about signing a non-disclosure agreement?'

'A what?' Trish still hadn't answered the previous question. Was the patient a baby, or maybe a toddler? Some kids could be diagnosed when they were really young.

Trish was looking a little shifty. She waved a piece of paper from the file. 'A non-disclosure agreement. You'd need to sign it.'

Now she was getting confused. What kind of job was

this? 'Why would I need to sign a non-disclosure? That seems a little odd. All nurses are bound by confidentiality anyway.'

'This is different. It's not a kid. It's an adult. And he's a well-known adult.'

Something had just clicked into place in her brain. 'Passport? Is the job not in the UK?'

Trish pushed the file across the desk towards Sam. 'The job is in Innsbruck, a ski resort in the Alps. You'd need to fly there tonight. And this is all the detail I have. I can't tell you any more. You sign the non-disclosure and leave tonight. You don't find out who you're working for until you get there.'

Alarm bells started ringing in her head. 'What do you mean?' She scanned the piece of paper in front of her. It looked as if it had come from some sort of agent. And it was only the basics. An adult male, diagnosed with diabetes less than forty-eight hours ago. Assistance required in helping him learn to manage and deal with his condition over the next three weeks.

Her gaze reached the bottom of the page. The fee. For three weeks' work. Her eyes were nearly out on sticks. How much??

'Is this safe?' Her voice squeaked.

She was trying to think rational thoughts, even though her brain was moving to rapid calculations of exactly how many months' worth of nursing-home fees that sum would cover.

It was all her own fault. When her mother had had the stroke over two years ago she'd spent the first few months trying to care for her mum herself. When it had become clear that she couldn't care for her mum and work at the same time, she'd changed jobs, swapping from a sister in an ITU, working shifts, to a school nurse with more regular and shorter hours. But the pay cut hadn't helped, particu-

larly when she'd had to pay two mortgages and supple-
mentary day care for her mother. And when the day-care
assistants had failed to show for the seventh time and her
mum had had an accident at home, she'd finally faced up
to the fact that her mother needed to be in a home.

Picking a nursing home that was up to her standards
hadn't been easy—and when she'd finally found one, the
fees were astronomical. But her mother was happy, and
well cared for, hence the reason she needed to work for the
agency to supplement her salary.

Trish stood up. 'Of course it's safe, Samantha. I wouldn't
send you anywhere you need to worry about. Now, can you
be on a flight out of Gatwick at seven tonight?' She held
out the non-disclosure agreement again, along with a pen.

Sam hesitated for only a second. How bad could this be?
It was probably some aging actor who needed some basic
guidance and hand-holding for a few weeks. She'd heard
of Innsbruck before—hadn't the Winter Olympics been
held there? The money was just too good to turn down.
She grabbed the pen and scribbled her signature before
she started asking any more questions that might make
her change her mind.

She stood up. 'Innsbruck—that's Austria, isn't it?' She
wrapped her scarf back around her head, trying to ignore
the fact that she and skiing didn't mix. She shot Trish a
beaming smile and held out her hand to shake it. 'A ski resort at Christmas? What more could a girl want? This'll
be a piece of cake.'

Mitchell Brody felt terrible. He wasn't even going to look
in the mirror because then he'd know that he looked terrible too.

The timing couldn't be worse. This was the last thing
he needed right now. His tour kicked off in three weeks.

He had to be fit and well for that. He needed to be able to perform. He had to get this under control.

The consultant was still shaking his head and frowning. 'You can't sign a discharge against medical advice. I won't allow it.'

Mitchell planted his hands on his hips. 'You can't stop me. Find me someone who can get me through this.'

'I've already put in a call to an agency in London. But it's a difficult time of year, staff are at a premium, and it will be hard to find someone with the skills you'll require.'

He sighed, frustration was building in his chest. 'Just find me someone, anyone, who can do this for me. I can pay. Money isn't a problem.'

The consultant narrowed his gaze. 'You don't understand. This isn't about someone "doing this" for you. You have to do it for yourself. You have to learn to take care of yourself with this condition. This is twenty-four hours a day, for the rest of your life. And it isn't an issue of cost. At this time of year staff come at a premium price. You have no choice but to pay it.'

Mitchell threw up his hands. 'I get it. I just don't have time for it. Not now. I'll learn about it later. I'll take the time then—in six months when this tour is over.'

'No.' The consultant folded his arms across his chest. 'If you don't do as I ask for the next three weeks, I'll notify your tour insurers. You won't be covered.'

For the second time in two days Mitchell was shocked. He wasn't used to people saying no to him. He was used to snapping his fingers and everyone doing exactly as he said. That was the joy of being a world-famous rock star. Once you earned beyond a certain point, people just didn't say no any more.

He could almost feel the blood draining from his body— as if he didn't feel sick enough already. 'You wouldn't do that.' His voice cracked as he spoke. This nightmare was just getting worse and worse. First the weeks of feeling like death warmed over. Then the ill-timed diagnosis of diabetes. Now a threat to his tour.

'I would, you know.' The consultant's chin was set with a determined edge. Mitchell recognised the look because he so frequently wore it himself. 'A sick rock star is no insurer's dream. You need to be healthy and in control to take part in the tour. To be frank, I don't think three weeks of specialist care is going to cut it. Even then, you'll need additional support on your tour. If you can't even adhere to the first set of guidelines I give you, then...' He let his voice tail off.

Mitchell's stomach was churning. It wasn't as if he wasn't rich already. But this tour had been planned for two years. The proceeds were going towards the funding of the children's hospital in this area. He'd supported it for years—but always on the condition that no one knew. The last thing he needed was the press invading the one part of his life that was still private. His funding had kept the children's hospital afloat for the last ten years. But things had changed. The building couldn't be repaired any more, the whole place needed to be rebuilt. And why rebuild anything half-heartedly? The plans had been drawn up and approved for a brand-new state-of-the-art facility. All they needed was the guaranteed cash. That's why he couldn't let them down—no matter how sick he was.

'Fine. I'll do it. Just find me someone.' He walked away in frustration and started stuffing his clothes into a holdall.

The consultant gave him a nod and disappeared down the corridor, coming back five minutes later. 'You're in luck. The agency called, they've found you a nurse. Her qualifications are a little unusual but she's got the experience we need.'

'What does that mean?'

'It means she'll be able to help you manage your condition. I'll send her some written instructions by email.' He glanced at his watch. 'She'll be on a flight out of Gatwick at seven tonight. She'll be here around eleven p.m.' He pointed to the packed bag. 'I'm not happy about discharging you until her plane lands.'

Mitchell shook his head and picked up the case with his injector pen. 'You've taught me how to do the injections. I take ten units tonight before I eat.' Then he pointed to another pen on the bedside table. 'And twenty-six units of that one before I go to bed. I get it. I do. Now, let me go. The nurse will be here in a few hours and I'll be fine until then.'

He could see the hesitation on the guy's face. It had only been two days and he was sick of the sight of this place already. Hospitals weren't much fun, even if you had the money to pay for a private room.

He tried his trademark smile. 'Come on. How much trouble can I get into in a few hours?'

The plane journey had been a nightmare. The man next to her had snored and drooled on her shoulder from the second the plane had taken off until it had landed in Innsbruck. She'd been doing her best to concentrate on the info she'd downloaded onto her tablet about the latest types of insulin and pumps. She wasn't sure what kind of regime her patient would be on but she wanted to have some background knowledge on anything she might face.

Her phone pinged as soon as she hit the tarmac. Great. An email from the doctor with detailed instructions. She struggled to grab her case from the revolving carousel and headed to the exit. She would have time to read the email on the journey to her hotel.

She scanned the arrivals lounge. Her heart gave a little jump when she saw a card with her name: 'Samantha Lewis'. It was almost like being a pop star.

She trundled her case over to the guy in the thick parka.

It was late at night and his hat was coated with thick snow-flakes. There was something so nice about being in a place covered with snow at Christmastime. Even if it was bitterly cold.

'Samantha Lewis?' He grabbed the handle of her case as she nodded. 'Is this it? Just one case?'

She grinned. 'Why? How many should I have brought?'

His face broke into a wide smile as he shook his head. 'Last time I picked someone up here she had ten suitcases, including one for her dog.'

'You can't be serious.'

He nodded. 'No kidding.' He had another look around. 'No skis?'

She shook her head. 'I'm here to work, not to ski.'

The guy's brow wrinkled. 'Hmm. Sorry.' He held out his hand. 'I'm Dave, Mitchell's sidekick. You name it, I do it.' He started to walk towards the exit. 'I've got a jacket and hat for you in the car.' His eyes skimmed up and down her body. 'It might be a little big but it's definitely your colour. I know you were called at short notice and we were worried you wouldn't have any gear with you.'

She tilted her head to the side. 'Who is Mitchell? I've not been told who I'm working for yet. And gear for what?'

An icy blast hit them as soon as they walked through the airport doors. Her grey duffel coat was no match for the winter Alpine temperatures. How nice. They'd bought her a coat and hat. She wasn't quite sure whether to be pleased or insulted.

He raised the boot on a huge black four-by-four and pushed her case inside. It was the biggest one she owned but it looked tiny in there. She blinked as she noticed the winter tyres and snow chains. Just how deep was the snow around here? He opened the door for her and she climbed inside. On the seat behind her was a bright blue ski jacket, slightly longer in style so it would cover her bum, alongside a matching pair of salopettes, hat, gloves and flat fur-lined black boots.

Her fingers brushed the skin of the jacket. It felt expensive. Thickly padded but light to touch.

Dave climbed into the driver's seat and nodded at the gear. 'Told you it was your colour. It matches your eyes.'

She blushed. Her eyes were the one thing that most people commented on. She wasn't sure whether being blonde-haired and blue-eyed was a blessing or a curse.

Dave started the car and pulled out of the parking lot, heading towards the main road. It felt like being in another world. They were surrounded by snow-covered Alps. The lights were glowing in the town in front of them. It looked warm and inviting against the black fir trees and high mountains.

'So, you haven't told me. Who do you work for?'

Dave's eyes flitted sideways for a second to look at her then focused back on the road ahead. 'No one's told you?' There was a knowing smile on his face.

She shrugged. 'Not yet. But I thought I was going to have to sign the non-disclosure in blood.'

'You're lucky you didn't.' She was joking, but he made it sound as if he heard that every other day.

'What's the big secret?' Curiosity was beginning to kill her. She hadn't given it much thought on the plane flight over, she'd been too busy focusing on the diabetes aspects and developing plans for a newly diagnosed adult patient. Plus, she still had that email to read. She glanced at her phone. Her 3G signal had left her. She had no idea what phone signals would be like in the Alps. She would have to ask for wifi access when they reached the hotel.

'Mitchell Brody. He's the big secret. He's just been diagnosed and he starts a world tour in three weeks. The timing couldn't be worse.'

Her mouth fell open and her heart did a little stop-start.

So not what she was expecting to hear. 'Mitchell Brody? *The* Mitchell Brody?' Now she understood the need for a non-disclosure agreement. Mitchell Brody, rock star, was pure media fodder. Every time the man blinked it practically made the news. Roguishly handsome, fit body and gorgeous smile. But he was the original bad boy. The papers were full of stories about him waking other guests in hotels by rehearsing at four in the morning. Huge headlines about bust-ups between band members and managers. Wrecked rooms and punch-ups with other stars were everyday news. Whoever was the model of the moment, was usually the woman photographed on his arm. He was worth millions, no, *billions*.

Dave shrugged. 'Is there any other?'

She gulped. The neat plan she'd imagined in her head instantly scrambled. Mitchell Brody wasn't the kind of guy who'd take kindly to planning all his meals and insulin doses. He lived by the seat of his pants. The guy had never played by the rules in his life—chances were, he wasn't about to start now.

She sagged back against her seat as she realised just what she was taking on. 'Wow. I didn't expect it to be him.'

Dave seemed amused. 'Who did you think it would be?'

'Honestly? I had no idea. Maybe some kind of TV soap actor or rich businessman. Mitchell Brody, well, he's just huge.' She looked out of the window at the passing streetlights. The shops were full of Christmas decorations and the buildings lined above were vintage façades of eighteenth-century houses in multicoloured pastel shades of pink, blue, yellow and peach. It was like summer, in the middle of winter. Gorgeous.

The car turned up a mountain. 'What hotel are we staying in? Do you think I'll be able to speak to the chef?'

Dave frowned. 'What makes you think we're staying in a hotel?'

She watched as they started up the mountain range, passing Tirol-styled hotel after hotel. 'Isn't that where everyone stays?'

'Maybe everyone who isn't Mitchell Brody. He's owned a house up here for the last five years.'

'He has?' The snow was glistening around them. The hotels were gorgeous—so picturesque. All set perfectly on the mountainside for easy access to the Innsbruck snow slopes. She shifted a little uncomfortably in her seat. Snow slopes. The signs were everywhere. Why else would anyone buy a house up here? She wrinkled her nose, she couldn't remember any of the press stories being about Mitchell's antics on the snow slopes. Nope, those stories were all about Caribbean retreats and private yachts. She cleared her throat. 'Does Mitchell like to ski, then?'

Dave laughed. 'Does Mitchell like to ski? Do bees flock around honey? Does some seventeen-year-old try and sweet-talk her way past me at every venue we go to?' He shook his head and gestured towards the back seat. 'Why do you think I brought you the ski gear?'

'To stop me from getting cold?' Her voice squeaked as she spoke, as the true horror of the situation started to unload. Her one and only skiing trip as a teenager had resulted in her spending most of her time flat on her back—or face down in the snow. Water had seeped through her jeans and down the sleeves and neck of her jacket. She'd finally hidden back down at the ski centre in front of a roaring fire with a hot chocolate in front of her. When the ski instructor had eventually come looking for her to persuade her back onto the slopes, her answer had been a resounding no.

Even the thought of skiing sent a shiver down her spine, which Dave misinterpreted. 'Better put your jacket on, we'll be there in a minute and it's freezing out there.'

She nodded and wiggled her arms out of her grey duffel and pulled the blue jacket over from the back seat. It was

pure and utter luxury, evident from the second she pushed
her arms inside. Even though they were still inside the car,
the heat enfolded her instantly. She tucked her blonde curls
under the matching woolly hat and pulled up the zip. 'It's
lovely, Dave. Thanks very much.'

She eyed the salopettes still lying across the back seat.
It was a stand-off. No way was she putting those on.

Dave turned the wheel down a long private road. The
warm glow at the end gradually came into focus. A beautiful, traditionally styled Tirol chalet. Okay, maybe it was
four times the size of all the others she'd seen. But it was
gorgeous, right down to the colourful window boxes, upper
balcony and black and red paintwork on the outside.

She opened the car door and almost didn't notice the
blast of icy air all around her. She was too busy staring at
the mountain house. She climbed out and automatically
stuck her hands in her pockets. The wind started whis-
tling around her jeans. Maybe salopettes weren't such a
bad idea after all.

'This place is huge,' she murmured. 'How many people
stay here?'

Dave was pulling her case from the trunk as if it was as
light as a feather. 'Just you and Mitchell.'

She sucked in a deep breath. The air was so cold it almost smarted against her throat. So not what she'd expected
to hear. 'You don't stay here too?'

Dave laughed. 'Me? No.'

'And he doesn't have any staff?' She was trying not to
think the thoughts that were currently circulating in her
brain. Alone. In a mountain retreat. With a gorgeous rock
star. She could almost hear her friend Carly's voice in her
ear, along with the matching action punch in the air. 'Kerch-
ing!'

This was really happening.

Wow. Her feet were stuck to the ground. Snow seeped

instantly through her flat-heeled leather boots, which had distinctly slippery soles. She should really move, but the whole place looked like a complete ice rink. She wobbled as she turned around and grabbed the fur-lined boots from the car. They had thick treads—obviously designed for places like this. It only took a minute to swap them over.

'Don't believe everything you read in the papers.' Dave strode over towards the entranceway of the house. 'Mitch is really private. He doesn't like people hanging around him. There's no cook. No PA.' He gave a little laugh as if he'd just realised what she'd be up against. 'Yeah, good luck with all this, Samantha.'

She blinked. She was going to be staying in a house *alone* with Mitchell Brody. The hottest guy on the planet. She might even have had a tiny crush on him at some point.

She might have lingered over some picture of him on the internet, showing off a naked torso with a fabulous set of abs, slim-fitting leather trousers and his shaggy, slightly too-long dark hair. The guy made grunge sexy.

She gulped. Her throat had never felt so dry. When was the last time she'd had something to drink? It must have been on the plane a few hours ago. Dave pushed open the door to the house and she stepped inside.

Wow. It was like stepping inside a shoot for a house magazine. The biggest sitting room she'd ever been in, white walls, light wooden floors, with a huge television practically taking up one wall. Sprawling, comfortable sofas and a large wooden dining-room table surrounded by twelve chairs. It screamed space. It yelled money. This place must have cost a fortune.

There was a tinkle of glass breaking off to her right, followed by some colourful language. Dave's brow wrinkled. 'Mitch?'

The headlines started to shoot through her brain. *Please don't let her first meeting be with a drunken rock star.*

She followed Dave as he strode through to the equally large kitchen. It should have been show home material too, but it was in complete disarray. Every door was hanging open, with food scattered everywhere. The door of the biggest refrigerator she'd ever seen was also open and Mitchell Brody was rummaging around inside—a glass of orange juice smashed around his feet. He didn't even seem to have noticed.

She glanced at Dave, whose face showed utter confusion at the scene around him. Every part of her body started to react. She moved quickly. 'Is this normal, Dave?'

'No, not at all.' He hadn't budged. His feet seemed welded to the floor.

Her instincts kicked into gear. She had no idea what to expect. She knew next to nothing about Mitchell Brody— only what she'd read in the press. But right now he wasn't Mitchell Brody, rock star. He was Mitchell Brody, patient. One who was newly diagnosed with diabetes. 'Is anyone else here?'

Dave shook his head. There was no one she could ask for some background information. Dave had been with her for the last hour, so Mitchell must have been alone. She hadn't even had a chance to read the email from the consultant yet. She strongly suspected his actions were to do with his diabetes but, then again, she might just be about to witness a legendary Mitchell Brody tantrum. No matter what, it was time to act.

She moved over next to him, kicking the glass away from around his feet and touching his back. 'Mitchell, can I help you with something?'

He spun around and she drew in a deep breath in shock. His shirt was hanging open and the top button of his jeans was undone. His face was gaunt, the frame under his shirt thin and the six-pack that adorned teenage walls had vanished, all clinical signs of ketoacidosis. Just how long had it taken them to diagnose him?

'Who are you?' he growled, before ignoring her completely and turning back to the refrigerator and scattering some more food around. An apple flew past her ear, closely followed by a banana, and then a jar of jam, which shattered on the grey tile floor.

The look in his eyes told her everything she needed to know. Mitchell Brody was having a hypoglycaemic attack, his blood sugar so low he would probably pass out in the next few minutes if she didn't get some food into him.

'Move,' he hissed, as he nudged her with his hip. She looked around. She had no idea where anything was in this place. She recognised the belligerent edge to his voice. Her sister had had it frequently as she'd hypoed as a child. That fine line where she hadn't been able to focus or steady her thoughts and had moved into auto-protect mode. It was almost as if the adrenaline fight-or-flight reaction had kicked in and it had been survival of the fittest.

'What does he like to eat?' she asked Dave, as she started searching through the cupboards for something suitable. She needed something to give him a quick blast of sugar in his system.

Dave hesitated. 'Strawberries and apples—he has a smoothie every morning. Or he did, until this happened.'

She reached past Mitchell, who was still fumbling in the refrigerator. 'Get him over to the sofa.' Her words were brisk. She had to act quickly. She grabbed a punnet of strawberries from the fridge and some apples. The blender was sitting on the countertop and she threw the whole lot in and held down the lid while pressing the button. She pulled a carton of yoghurt from the fridge too. It was peach, totally random, but it would have to do. She dumped it in the blender as well and kept pressing. Dave appeared at her side, putting his hands on Mitchell's shoulders and guiding him over to sit down. 'What's going on?'

'His blood sugar is too low. If I can get something into him quickly, he should be fine,' she said over the noise of the blender.

She grabbed a glass from one of the open cupboards and dumped the contents of the blender into it. There were some straws scattered across the countertop and she pushed a couple into the drink. Seconds later she sat down on the sofa next to him.

'Hi, Mitchell, I'm Samantha, your nurse. Can you take a little drink of this for me, please?'

She held the straw up towards his lips and he immediately batted it away with his hands. 'No, leave me alone.' Her stomach was doing flip-flops. Every person was different, but from past experience her sister could also be slightly aggressive while hypoing. Not an ideal scenario. Particularly with a man who had more muscle than she did. Thank goodness Dave was here. Maybe he would respond better to a familiar face?

She held tightly on to the glass and persisted, 'It's your favourite. Just take a sip.'

His eyes had that slightly wild look in them, definitely unfocused as if the world around him wasn't making sense. He hesitated for a second, before finally taking a reluctant sip. After a few moments he sucked a little harder, as if he'd recognised the taste of what he was drinking. He grabbed the glass from her hand and held it close to his chest while he sucked.

It was a slow process, but one that Samantha was familiar with. She was patient, she could wait. Five minutes later the glass was nearly drained. Her hands were itching to find a blood-glucose monitor and check his levels—there had to be one around here somewhere. But she didn't want to leave his side.

Dave was looking pretty uncomfortable. He clearly wasn't used to anything like this and it was obvious she was going to have to give him a few lessons in dealing with diabetes too.

'What do we do now?' he asked.

'Now?' She sat back against the sofa. It was every bit as comfortable as it looked. 'Now, Dave, we wait.'

CHAPTER TWO

THERE WAS AN angel floating around in his vision. An angel with blonde curls, bright blue eyes and a matching jacket. She also had a weird matching hat on her head that made the curls look as if they were suspended in mid-air. Strange. His dreams didn't normally look like this.

The angel kept patting his hand and talking to him quietly. Those weren't the normal actions of a woman this hot in his dreams either. Maybe he was turning over a new leaf?

He smiled to himself. Maybe he could take his dream in another more Mitch-like direction?

There was another voice in the background. It was annoying him. Eating into the little space in his head that was cloudy and comfortable. But something else wasn't comfortable. His back ached. And for some odd reason he felt cold.

His hands touched his bare chest. Why was he half-dressed?

He sat up, trying to unload the fuzzy feeling around him. Ahh. He recognised that voice. The background noise was Dave. He was talking the way he did when he was nervous, too fast, his words all joined up and practically rolling into one.

The blue angel was still misting around. She was talking to him again. 'Hi, there, Mitchell. Are you back with us?'

She didn't wait for a reply—just as well really, as his mouth felt a bit thick—as if someone had just punched him and given him a split lip. He stuck his tongue out and licked. No, no blood. But there was definitely something else, something familiar. Strawberries. When had he eaten those?

His brain was starting to function again. Tiny little jigsaw pieces slotting into place to give a bigger picture.

But one thing was still standing out a mile. The unfamiliar.

She touched him again. Only on his arm, but it was enough to make his senses spark. Contrary to public belief, Mitchell Brody didn't like people touching him, pawing at him. It made him feel as if he were for sale. Like a cashmere scarf or leather shoe being stroked in a women's department store. Yuck.

He shrugged her off and sat up. 'Who are you?' He shook his head, it felt like jelly was in his brain.

She smiled. A beaming white, perfect-teeth kind of smile. Who was her dentist?

She held her hand out towards him. 'You've been expecting me. I'm Samantha Lewis, your nurse. The agency sent me to help you manage your diabetes.' The smile disappeared from her face. 'And not a moment too soon. Why did they discharge you from hospital before I got here?'

A frown creased her forehead, ruining the smooth skin and showing little creases around her eyes. He'd liked her better before.

He moved in the chair, turning around to see the mumbling Dave.

'Dave, what's going on here?' His voice sounded a little funny. A little slow. His eyes took in the chaos in the kitchen, which looked as if food had exploded all around it. He stood up and pointed. 'And what on earth happened in my kitchen?'

The last thing he could remember was looking at the

clock and wondering when his nurse would arrive. He hadn't even decided what room to put her in.

His shirt was flapping around and he did up a few of the buttons haphazardly. Not that he was embarrassed by his body. The amount of calendars he sold every year put paid to that idea. But it was hardly an ideal meeting with his new nurse. When had she got here?

New nurse. Now his brain was kicking back into gear he was more than a little surprised. He had kind of expected some older matron-type who'd bark orders at him for the next three weeks.

He certainly hadn't expected some cute, slim, blonde-haired, blue-eyed chocolate-box-type cheerleader. In lots of ways he should be pleased.

But he wasn't. Not really. Something wasn't right. Was this what the doctor had warned him about? How sometimes with diabetes you could be unwell?

After tonight's display he needed someone to get his condition under control so he could start on his tour. People were counting on him. Kids were counting on him—not to mention their families. The last thing he needed was some bright-eyed, bushy-tailed young girl hanging around him, distracting him.

She tapped him on the arm. The expression on her face had changed. She wasn't all smiles now. She was deadly serious. 'Mitchell, can you tell me where your blood-glucose meter is? You need to check your levels then we'll have a chat about what just happened.'

She spoke to him as if he was a child. Her tone and stance had changed completely.

So Mitchell did what he always did. He completely ignored her and walked over to the kitchen, crunching on some broken glass on the tiled floor. 'Who broke a glass?' he yelled, spinning around to accuse Dave and the strange new nurse.

He held his hands out. 'What happened, Dave? Who did it? Who's been in my kitchen?' He didn't like disorder. That's why it was so much easier staying by himself—there was no one else around to make a mess.

Dave was pushing things back into cupboards. He turned around and rested his hands behind him on the countertop, hesitating before he spoke.

'Well, actually, I wasn't here. I went to pick up Samantha at the airport. And when we got back...' His voice tailed off as if he didn't want to finish.

Mitchell could feel his exasperation reach breaking point. He had no idea what was going on in his own home. 'When you got back, what?' He glanced at the clock and blinked, then looked again. The last two hours of his life seemed to have vanished without him knowing where they'd gone.

Dave laid a hand on his shoulder. 'You were raking about the cupboards and the fridge. We weren't quite sure what you were doing.'

It was as if the final piece of the jigsaw puzzle fell into place. Except it didn't slot in quietly, it slammed in, as if banged by a hammer. Realisation dawned on his face and he looked around again. 'I did this?'

Samantha appeared at his side. 'Mitchell, it's time you and I had a talk.'

This time he erupted. 'I don't want to talk! I want to know what the hell happened here!'

But his nurse didn't jump at his outburst. She didn't seem at all surprised. She just folded her arms across her chest as if she were some kind of immovable force. 'From this point onwards you do exactly what I tell you. If I tell you we're going to talk then...' she paused '...we're *going to talk.*' She pointed over towards the sofa. 'So get your butt over there, Mr Brody, and sit down!'

The heat in the kitchen was stifling. Samantha yanked

off her goose-down jacket and flung it over a chair. If she kept this on much longer she would be roasted like a chicken. Her face must be scarlet by now.

This was definitely a baptism of fire. She looked at the clock—it was almost midnight and Dave had already told her he didn't stay in the house. 'Dave, why don't you go on home to bed? I'll be fine. I'll need to talk to you in the morning though, it's important you understand how to deal with things.'

Dave gave a grateful nod and disappeared out of the door as if he were being chased by a herd of zombies. All of this was definitely new to him.

Mitchell hadn't moved—probably from the shock of someone talking to him like that. What was she thinking? But she was his nurse. It was her job to take charge. 'Mitchell, your blood-glucose meter, where is it?' He was in shock, she could tell. It looked like he'd just experienced his first full-blown hypoglycaemic attack and was totally confused.

After a few seconds he turned to face her.

Wow. He was just inches from her, and Samantha had just experienced the full Brody effect—those dark brown eyes and perfect teeth. It didn't matter that his face was gaunter than normal and his body leaner. Teenagers all over the world would give their eye-teeth to be in this position. She was trying not to focus on the bare skin on his chest and scattered dark hair beneath the loosely fastened shirt. Trying not to lower her gaze to get another look at his abs.

She was beginning to feel a little hot and bothered again. He hadn't moved. His brown eyes were fixed on hers. Sucking her in and making her forget what she was supposed to be doing. What on earth was he thinking?

Then he blinked.

He pointed over to a blue plastic box nestled behind the sofa. 'It's there.'

The moment was completely lost and Sam mentally kicked herself.

It snapped her back into focus. She was here to do a job. Here to get this man well again. She couldn't stand around, mooning like some teenager. It was embarrassing.

She walked over, picked up the box and gestured to him to sit down again, but he shook his head and moved over towards the huge dining table instead.

As the minutes progressed he was getting more and more back to normal—whatever Mitchell Brody's normal might be. The dining table was more formal than lounging on the sofa. She was kind of annoyed she hadn't thought of it herself. She had to keep this on a professional level.

He slumped down into one of the chairs, his handsome face skewed by a puzzled frown. It wasn't familiar. She'd never seen a picture of him looking so dejected. It made things crystal clear for her. She had to take rock star Mitchell Brody, and what she knew of him, out of this equation.

This was a twenty-nine-year-old guy who'd just been diagnosed with a life-changing disease—and by the look of his body the diagnosis had taken a long time.

She reached out and touched his hand before she spoke. He flinched a little at her touch. 'Mitchell, I'm going to help you with this. Everything will be fine. It's still early days. We've got three weeks to try and help you get a handle on your condition.'

He groaned and shook his head. 'I don't have time for this right now. I've got a tour starting soon. I need to focus all my energy and attention on that.'

She squeezed his hand but he pulled it away again. He clearly didn't like being touched—she'd have to remember that. It was plain he had a lot on his mind, but she had to bring him back to the immediate future. 'No, Mitchell. You have to focus on *this*. If you don't, there won't be any tour, because you won't be able to perform.'

'I won't?' It was almost as if his stronghold tower was wobbling all around him and about to come crashing down. There was real confusion on his face and it was the first time she'd seen him look a bit vulnerable. Maybe Dave was right, maybe she shouldn't believe what was in the press.

She flipped open the box and pulled out the blood-glucose meter. Although there were numerous kinds on the market, they were all very similar. She handed it to him. 'Let's start at the very beginning.' She gave a little smile. 'A very good place to start. I take it someone at the hospital showed you how to do this?'

He smiled, and opened his meter. 'Yeah, Dragon Lady was very bossy.' His head tilted to the side. 'Shouldn't you be doing this for me? Isn't that why you're here?'

The words were said more curiously than accusingly but it made her realise it was time to be very clear about what her role was.

'This is your condition, Mitchell, not mine. You need to learn how to manage it.' She held out her hands towards the still messy kitchen. 'We can't let things like this happen all the time. You need to learn how to control things. No one else can do it for you.'

She bit her lip. She was praying he wasn't about to have a monster-style, rock-star temper tantrum on her and start ordering her around. It would be so easy to tell him what to eat, check his blood-sugar levels and tell him what insulin to take, but it wasn't safe. He had to learn how to do all that by himself.

Children as young as five were taught how to manage their diabetes. And for all Mitchell was a millionaire rock star, he was still an adult with a condition that needed to be controlled.

She gave a little smile. She had the strangest feeling that Mitchell Brody wouldn't take kindly to being told what to do anyway. She was probably going to have to tiptoe around him.

He zipped open the fabric case and pulled out the meter, slotting a testing strip into place. The meter turned on automatically and she watched as he hesitated just for a second before placing the automatic finger-pricking device over the pad of one of his fingers. Seconds later he put a tiny drop of blood on the testing strip and the machine started its ten-second countdown.

Samantha said nothing. She just watched. He'd obviously paid attention when Dragon Lady had shown him how to use this and he seemed to manage it with no problems. One less thing to worry about.

The machine beeped and she looked at the reading. Four point two. She pointed at the screen. 'Do you know what a normal blood-sugar reading is?'

He nodded and sighed. 'It's supposed to be between four and seven, but mine was much higher than that in hospital.' She wanted to smile. He could obviously remember what he'd been told. Things were beginning to look up.

'It would have been. You'd just been diagnosed with diabetes. It takes a bit of time to regulate things.'

He leaned back in the chair. She could see the release of pent-up muscles, the fatigue that was common after a hypoglycaemic attack, practically hitting him like a wrecking ball. 'So what now, genius?' One eyebrow was raised.

It was too late to do anything but the basics right now and she had to prioritise because it was clear he needed to rest. She stood up and walked over to the kitchen, rummaging around to find some bread and pop it in the toaster that had probably cost more than her car.

'Right now we're going to give you something else to eat. Although your blood sugar is in the normal range, you've probably been running a bit higher than normal for the last few days. It makes you more prone to hypo attacks.

The smoothie will have given you a burst of sugar—the last thing we want is for that to fall rapidly in the middle of the night. I'm making you something a bit more substantial to eat.' She glanced in the fridge. 'Cheese or ham on your toast?'

Both eyebrows went up this time. 'You're making me something to eat?'

She wagged her finger at him as the toast popped. 'This is a one-off. My priority is to get you safely through the night. I take it you've still to take your long-acting insulin?'

He scrunched up his face. 'Yeah.'

'Then you can do it after this. We'll talk in the morning about how best to handle things going forward.' She leaned back into the fridge and came back out with cheese in one hand and ham in the other. 'You didn't say which you prefer.'

'Ham, with a little mustard on the side.' She nodded and quickly made up the sandwich. 'We need to talk about food choices tomorrow,' she said, as she sat the plate down in front of him.

He groaned. 'Colour me happy.'

A smile broke across her face. 'Wow. I haven't heard that in years. My grandpa used to say that all the time.'

For a second something changed. The barrier that had been between them from the second she'd got there seemed to disappear. This time his smile reached right up into his weary eyes.

He wasn't the sexy guy whose calendar had adorned the staffroom wall at work. He wasn't the heartthrob who'd played sold-out venues around the world.

He was just Mitchell Brody, the guy she was alone with in a million-pound chalet in the snowy Alps. Right now she was living every girl's dream. Honestly? What nurse did she know who wouldn't kill for this job?

Which was why it made her feel so uncomfortable.

Up close and personal he had the kind of warm brown eyes that could just pull you in and keep you there. The kind that could make you forget everything else around you. And that was pretty much what was happening now.

The meter gave a little beep—reminding them to switch it off—and it jerked her from her daydreams. 'Cup of tea?'

She started boiling the kettle and searched through the cupboards for cups. He was still watching her with those eyes and it was unnerving. His gaze seemed to linger on her behind as she bent down to look in a few cupboards before he finally said, 'Top right for tea, bottom left for cups,' and took another bite of his sandwich. 'To be honest, though, I'd prefer a beer.'

Her brain switched straight into professional mode. 'It's too soon for a beer.' The words came out automatically before she could stop them and she cringed. He was a rock star—of course he'd want a beer. She had to try and push her bossy instincts aside and be realistic and put the patient first.

It was no use telling people who were newly diagnosed what they couldn't or shouldn't do. For most people, it just gave them the urge to rebel or to think their life would never be the same. And that could be disastrous. She'd seen exactly how her sister had reacted to things like that.

No. She knew better. This was all about making this work for the patient. This was his life, not hers. She was beginning to question her suitability for this job. It would always be tricky to teach an adult about something they might consider a new way of life. But to teach someone like Mitchell Brody? It seemed like an almost impossible task.

She watched as he ran his fingers through his just-too-long, messy hair. The man didn't know how damn sexy he was. Then again, with the press and media attention he got, he probably did. Working with this guy was going to be more than distracting. Living in the same house as him?

She would have to bolt her door at night and only hope that she didn't sleepwalk.

As there was no evidence of a teapot she poured the boiling water into the mugs, squeezing the tea bags out and adding milk. She put them on the table and took a deep breath, 'Don't worry. I'll talk you through what to do with your insulin and testing if you want to have a few beers.' She paused, choosing her words carefully. 'When the time is right.'

His hand moved slowly, lifting the mug and taking a sip. He cringed. 'I like two sugars in my tea.'

She smiled and grabbed her handbag, which had been abandoned on the table, rummaging around for a few seconds before pulling out a saccharin dispenser and clicking two into his cup.

He tried again. This time the grimace was even worse. 'That's disgusting!'

She shrugged. 'You'll adjust. In a few weeks you won't even notice the difference.'

'Is that a promise?' He held his cup up towards her.

She nodded and clinked her cup on his. This was about to get interesting.

He was still trying to come to terms with the events of the last hour. If anyone had told him a few weeks ago that he'd be sitting in Innsbruck, drinking tea with a hot chick around midnight, he would have laughed in their face.

Drinking tea was not what Mitchell Brody was known for. But the truth was it was actually about all he could face right now.

For the last few weeks leading up to his diagnosis he'd known something had been very wrong. He'd never felt so tired, both physically and mentally. He'd been beginning to question if he was feeling stressed about the tour. Which was why he'd ended up here, his favourite haunt in the world—and the one place the press hadn't figured out he owned yet.

His house in Mauritius was regularly buzzed by helicopters. The townhouse he owned in London practically had the press camped outside the front door, and as for the house in LA. Well, it was a stop on one of the 'houses of the stars' coach tours. Privacy was virtually impossible.

Which was why he loved Innsbruck so much. He'd bought the house ten years ago under his brother's name. Tucked up in the snowy Alps, with direct access to some of the best ski slopes in the world. Who could want to stay anywhere else?

He loved the area. He loved the people. Most of all he loved the staff at the nearby children's hospital. His family had stayed here for just over a year when he'd been six. His father had worked for one of the big pharmaceutical companies that had had business in Austria and the whole family had had to up sticks for a year.

It had been great for two young boys. They'd learned to ski within a few weeks and had never been off the slopes until his brother Shaun's diagnosis. Then they'd spent the rest of the time in and out of St Jude's Children's Hospital.

From the balcony at the front of the chalet he could even see the roof of St Jude's. It was part of the reason he'd jumped at the chance to build here. Although his house was chalet-style, the expansive size almost made a mockery of that description.

He loved it here. He really did. This was his hideaway. There were people here that knew him as Mitch, the boy whose brother had had leukaemia, and had known him for the last twenty or more years. Shaun's recovery had been a long process, and even after they'd moved from Austria his family had continued to holiday here twice a year.

Here, he wasn't Mitchell Brody, rock star. He wasn't the guy with four homes around the world and a dozen fast cars. He wasn't the guy who'd fallen out of one nightclub too many, or had needed to be bailed out of jail the next morning. He was just Mitch, who had to queue in the local bakery for his favourite pastry, like everyone else. And he liked it that way.

He liked somewhere to be normal. He liked to be around people who had no expectation of him—where he was just another guy. Somewhere along the line all that had been lost.

With girls too. He'd been the spotty teenager who'd just wanted his first kiss. The young guy who everyone had laughed at for locking himself in his room all the time to practise his guitar.

But practice made perfect. He was testament to that. His last album had achieved platinum status in a matter of hours, with women queuing round the block of the hotel he'd been staying in, hoping for a glimpse of him.

It was amazing what a few years of going to the gym, some filling out and a careless approach to haircuts could do.

But that didn't help with the girl sitting across the table from him right now, looking at him with those amazing blue eyes. He'd been so desperate to be discharged from hospital he couldn't have cared less what his nurse looked like. As long as she could get him through the next three weeks, that had been fine by him.

But he hadn't banked on this. He hadn't banked on her.

He squinted at her. 'What did you say your name was?'

She gave her head a little shake and laughed. 'Samantha. Samantha Lewis. I'm your nurse.'

He leaned back in his chair appreciatively. 'Oh, yes, you are.'

Her eyebrows arched and she wagged her finger at him. 'Don't start with me, sunshine. Don't you be giving me that kind of look. I'm here to do a job. That's all. I'm only staying up with you and making you tea so we can check your blood sugar before you go to bed.'

He leaned forward, planting his chin on his hand. 'Let's talk about this job. What *exactly* will you be doing for me?'

He watched her cheeks flush at the way he'd emphasised the word and the way she squirmed in her chair. He liked it. Samantha Lewis was different from the last lot of women he'd been involved with.

Right now, it felt like this diabetes diagnosis was a weight around his neck. Samantha Lewis might lighten the load a little.

'I'll be doing exactly what I should be doing. I'll be helping you monitor your blood-glucose levels, teaching you how to adjust your insulin and how to recognise the early signs of a hypoglycaemic attack. It's important you have good blood-glucose control. It'll help you stay independent and reduce the risk of any complications.'

He groaned. She might not look like Dragon Lady, but she was certainly beginning to sound like her.

'Let's talk about something else.' He leaned across the table towards her. 'Is there a Mr Lewis I should know about?'

Her body gave the slightest backward jerk, as if she was deciding how to answer the question. Then she took another sip of her tea and rolled her eyes at him. Her muscles relaxed a little, as if she was shaking off a little of her tension. 'Not that it's any of your business, but there's no Mr Lewis at present. I'm still interviewing possible contenders.'

Oh. He liked that. But she wasn't finished.

'So, Mitchell Brody—and is that your real name? — should I expect to find the latest female movie star or model hiding in the one of the cupboards in here?'

He grinned. A sparring partner. Samantha Lewis might even be fun. 'Yes, Mitchell Brody is my real name. And, no, there's no females hiding in cupboards, but I reserve the right for that to change.'

Something flitted across her eyes and the soft smile vanished in an instant. 'Are you expecting someone to join you soon?'

What was that? The tiniest spark of jealousy? He pushed the thought from his head in an instant. Ridiculous. She was his nurse. Nothing else. No matter how cute she looked.

'No.' He shook his head and held his hands out. 'To be honest, this place is my sanctuary. I've never brought a female...' he lifted his fingers in the air and made invisible quote marks '...*friend* back here. Dave's the only person you'll find sloping about. Oh, and the local maid service that comes in every day for a tidy up. That reminds me.' He stood up and walked over to the other side of the table where his phone lay.

'What are you doing?'

He scrolled through his messages. 'I got a text earlier and with everything that's happened I forgot to reply.' He looked around the room. 'What do you think? Red and gold? Blues and silver, or purples and pinks? No.' He gave a shudder at that last one.

'Red and gold for what?' She wrinkled her nose up again, it really did define the cute factor in her.

'The colour of the tree and Christmas decorations. The tree will come tomorrow, I just need to tell them what colours I want.' He looked around the sitting room. It really was looking kind of sparse. The tree and other decorations would give it a little warmth to match the fireplace that he'd forgotten to turn on.

'You get someone to bring you a tree and decorate it?'

He nodded. 'Yeah, every year. I just need to tell them what colours I want. What do you think?'

She shifted in her chair. 'Why are you asking me? It's your house, not mine.'

She was being a little frosty with him. He'd liked the version from a few minutes earlier. A sparring partner with some twinkle in her eye.

'Well, you're going to be here over Christmas too. I'd hate to pick something that made you shudder every time you walked in the door. I usually do this at the beginning of December, but with being ill and all I just kind of forgot about it.' He walked over to a big empty space next to the far wall. 'This is where the tree normally goes. They usually put some décor around the fireplace too.'

Her eyes narrowed as she looked around. 'It depends what you want. Red and gold would give some warmth to the place, but blue and silver would probably fit more with your white walls and pale floors.'

He sat down in the chair next to her and gave her a nudge in the ribs. 'Yeah, but which one would you *like*?'

He was teasing her again. Trying to goad that spark back into her eyes.

She gave a little sigh and took the last gulp of her tea. 'I think I'd probably like the red and gold best.' She hesitated. 'But you're missing out. Putting up the Christmas decorations is one of the best parts of Christmas. Getting someone else to do it for you?' She shook her head and glanced at her watch. 'Right, it's time to check your blood sugar again. If it's okay, you can do your night-time injection and go to bed. We'll have a chat about things in the morning.'

Something had just flickered past her eyes. A feeling of regret perhaps? It didn't matter how much he was paying Sam Lewis, she was still missing Christmas with her family to do this job. Maybe he should give that a little more thought?

He raised his eyebrows. 'You're giving me permission to go to bed?' He let out a little laugh. 'Well, that'll be a first.'

Her cheeks flushed again. She was easily embarrassed. It

might even be fun having her around for a few weeks. She might make having diabetes seem not so much like a drag.

He sat down and took a minute to retest himself, turning the monitor around to show her the result of eight. She nodded. 'It'll probably go up a little more as you digest your food. That's fine.' She stood up and walked over to the door where her suitcase was. 'Where will I be sleeping?'

Yikes. He hadn't even told her where her room was. Hospitality wasn't his forte. His mother would be furious with him. He moved quickly, grabbing the handle of her case and gesturing for her to follow him. 'Sorry, Samantha. You'll be down here.' He swung open the door to the room. It was at the front of the house and had views all the way down the valley. He heard her intake of breath as she looked out over the snowy landscape and bright orange lights from the streets a mile beneath them.

It gave him a little surge of pleasure that she was obviously impressed. He loved this place and wanted others to love it too. She'd walked over to the large glass doors that led out onto the balcony and pressed her hands against the glass. 'This is gorgeous.' She spun around. 'And the room is huge.'

He pointed to one side of her. 'Your bathroom is in here, and the walk-in closet behind you.'

He pulled open the door to the closet and she automatically walked inside. After a second she threw out her hands and spun around, laughing. 'Mitchell, this closet is bigger than my bedroom back home!'

The sparkle was definitely back in her eyes. And he liked it. 'I'm glad you like it.' He pointed to the wooden sleigh-style bed with the giant mattress. 'Sleep well, because we'll be up early in the morning.'

She looked a little surprised. Did she think he liked to lie in till midday? 'Okay. What time do you want to have breakfast?'

'Six.'

Her eyebrows shot up. 'Six? Why so early?'

This was probably her first time here. He hadn't even asked her if she'd been before. He winked at her. 'Because six is the best time to ski.'

CHAPTER THREE

SHE'D JUST SPENT the best night in the most luxurious bed she'd ever slept in. She couldn't even begin to imagine the thread count on these fabulous sheets but chances were she'd never experience them again. She was half-inclined to try and stuff them in her case as she was leaving.

But the best bit was the morning. She hadn't closed the curtains last night and as the sun had gradually risen over the snow-covered Alps she'd had the most spectacular view. The bedroom balcony looked directly out over the hillside to a blanket of perfect white snow. There was something so nice about lying in bed, all cosseted and cosy, admiring the breathtaking, snow-covered scenery.

No wonder Mitchell loved this place. He'd called it his sanctuary. And as the press were usually clamouring around him for a story she could see why the surrounding peace and quiet was so precious to him. She could quite easily fall in love with it herself.

Everything about this job should be perfect. Everything about this job *could* be perfect—if only she hadn't spent most of last night tossing and turning, fretting about Mitchell's parting comment.

Skiing.

The words sent a horrible shiver down her spine. He'd been joking, right? He had to be. No one had stipulated she had to be able to ski, because that would have been a deal-breaker for her. She couldn't even begin to pretend to be ski-slope-worthy. More importantly, she didn't want to be.

But what about the bright blue ski jacket and matching salopettes? Maybe she should have asked questions as soon as she'd seen them. Maybe she should have asked Dave for more information last night. But there hadn't really been a chance last night.

In the early morning light she peered at her watch. Nearly six. She felt wide-awake now, but she'd probably hit a wall by lunchtime today and need to lie down for an hour. Not ideal when she was supposed to be supervising Mitchell.

Mitchell Brody. She honestly couldn't believe it. She squeezed her eyes shut and resisted the temptation to pinch herself. Her skin was tingling just at the thought of the fact that somewhere in this sprawling house Mitchell Brody could be as partially dressed as she was. Hmm. Or maybe he was in the shower, water streaming over those lean abs...

She wanted to grab her phone and start texting all her friends, but she'd signed that non-disclosure agreement, plus the fact that as a nurse she couldn't talk about her patients.

Chances were she'd finish this job and never be able to tell anyone a thing about it. But no one could stop her imagination...

She'd never been in a situation like this before, itching to talk about something but having to stay quiet. It was weird.

There was a noise outside and her stomach gave a little flip-flop. There was only one other person in this house. He hadn't been kidding. It was almost exactly six and Mitchell Brody was up and around.

'Knock, knock.' The low, sexy voice nearly made her jump a foot in the air. Without waiting for an answer, the door creaked open and Mitchell stuck his head inside. She bolted upright in bed and pulled the covers up underneath her chin. This must be what mild shock felt like; her tongue was currently stuck to the roof of her mouth.

He was smiling, obviously feeling better. He didn't seem to notice her lack of response. 'Hi, there. Gorgeous view, isn't it?' She nodded in agreement. She could hardly disagree. Mitchell was looking bright and sparky and from what she could see was dressed for the slopes. She, on the other hand, was wearing next to nothing.

She was trying not to panic. The easiest thing in the world was to drop back into nurse mode. 'Have you checked your blood sugar this morning? What about breakfast?'

Nurse mode put her on autopilot and before she'd given herself a chance to think about it she threw back the thick duvet cover and bent forward to look for her slippers.

She heard a noise. His sharp intake of breath before she realised what she'd done. Her short red satin slip of a nightie had obviously just given him an eyeful. Her hand darted up to press against her cleavage, trying to keep the garment firmly in place. 'Oh... I, I need to put something else on.'

But what? She'd collapsed on the bed last night with hardly a chance to open her suitcase. Thankfully, her nightie had been on top. But she couldn't even see a glimpse of the underwear she desperately needed right now.

Mitchell had the good grace to look away. But she could see the smile plastered on his face. Yip. He'd definitely got an eyeful. 'There's a dressing gown in the en suite if that will help,' he murmured. 'But don't feel obliged on my account.'

The heat rushed to her cheeks. Six o'clock in the morning and he was starting with his trademark cheek. He was going to have to learn that Samantha Lewis was *not* a morning person.

She walked quickly to the en suite and found the white fluffy robe hanging behind the door. She shrugged it on and tied the belt around her waist, trying not to think if someone else had worn it before her. There. Better. Being covered gave her the confidence boost she needed. Mitchell Brody was usually surrounded by a bunch of skeletal supermodels. She was surprised he hadn't passed out at the sight of some more womanly curves. She was lucky, naturally slim with maybe a tiny trace of cellulite. But absolutely nowhere near a supermodel frame. He didn't need to like it, though, because all that mattered was how she did her job.

She took thirty seconds to brush her teeth and didn't even waste her time looking in the mirror. What was the point? He was still waiting at the doorway as she walked over and put her hands on her hips. 'Now, where were we?'

He shot her a sexy smile. 'You were trying to decide if you should get dressed around me.' The drawl of his voice sent her saliva glands into overload. If her mouth hadn't been firmly closed she would have drooled. She didn't speak. Just gave him what she thought was a haughty stare and raised her eyebrows.

He blinked. 'Blood sugar seven. I've had breakfast and taken my insulin. It's time to hit the slopes before it starts to get busy.' He waggled his finger at her. 'You'll have to get up earlier if you want breakfast here, Sam.'

Her stomach gave an automatic growl. She didn't like to miss breakfast and it felt like she was being reprimanded on her first day on the job. Cheeky sod.

'What did you eat for breakfast and how much insulin did you take?'

He frowned, his smile disappearing in an instant. 'I told you. My blood sugar is fine.' He glanced at his watch. 'I'm hitting the slopes. You can come if you want to. I'm not sure when I'll be back.'

She felt a wave of panic. There was no way she could hit the slopes next to him, but what if Mitch had a hypo while skiing? That could be disastrous.

'*No.*' It came out like a shout and she cringed inside. 'You're not ready to do anything like that. You need to wait a few more days until your blood-sugar levels are steadier. Then we'll talk about exercise and the effect it has on blood-sugar control, and what you need to do. You were only diagnosed a few days ago. It's far too soon.' Her voice was sounding much more authoritative than she actually felt. Her insides were curling up.

The furrows across his brow deepened, accompanied with a spark of fury in his eyes. 'Look, lady, I don't care what you say. The slopes are perfect and I won't be missing a second. If you want to watch me, come along. If you don't...' he pointed towards the still-warm bed '...feel free to go back to bed.'

He turned on his heel and left, leaving her to scuttle down the corridor after him in her bare feet. 'Mitchell, wait. I wasn't joking. Do you have food with you? Something to eat if you start to hypo on the slopes? Don't you realise how dangerous that could be for the other people around you?'

She was trying desperately to appeal to his sense of justice. Trying to make him slow down for a second. Trying anything to stop him heading for the slopes with her having to follow.

But Mitchell was a man on a mission. There was the briefest hesitation—as if he was giving some consideration to her words—before he clenched his jaw. Everything about him changed, his whole stance tense. The words were controlled but the strain was apparent. 'I'm done with this. See you on the slopes.'

He grabbed something from the countertop then threw open the door, bringing in an icy blast before he disappeared out into the swirls of freshly falling snow. She shouted after him, 'I'll meet you at the mid-station at seven!'

She took a few deep breaths as the skin prickled on her legs. The fluffy dressing gown was no match for the weather outside that currently circulated in chills around her pale skin. She slammed the door quickly, her brain frantic.

Should she throw on her clothes and try and follow him? Had he even heard her? Where on earth had he gone? She didn't even know the way to the ski slopes, let alone anything else.

Her eyes caught sight of what was lying on the counter. A packet of chocolate wafers, with a few missing. She smiled. She breathed the slightest sigh of relief. It might not be ideal, but it was something. He'd grabbed some before he'd left.

She made up her mind. She had the clothes. There were no excuses. She might not be able to ski, but she could be in and around the slopes. There was no way she could sit around here. Right now, she'd no idea if Mitchell intended to ski for an hour or all day.

And his attitude irked her. Mitchell Brody had a lot of learning to do. She flicked the switch on the kettle. The coffee machine looked inviting but she'd no idea how to work it. She'd investigate it later.

The clock on the wall showed six-fifteen. She could shower, dress and have a quick cup of tea before she left. Wherever Mitchell Brody had gone, she could find him.

She was used to dealing with teenager tantrums. A rock star in a bad mood? He would have nothing on those.

Suddenly there was huge boom. The noise was deafening and the glasses in the cupboards around her rattled. What now?

The air was perfect, crisp, clear and icy cold. The snow around him untouched—just waiting for that first winding ski track to mar its complexion. The ski conditions were better than he could've expected. It paid to have people in the know.

For a little extra cash he'd managed to persuade the cable-car operator to start early and he'd been up and down the Hafelekar slope twice. The Nordkette off-piste could be dangerous, with risk of avalanche and warnings posted everywhere stating the falls could be fatal.

But Mitchell knew these slopes like the back of his hand. He enjoyed mornings like this. Most days at this time it was only the die-hard skiers on the slopes. The thunderous detonations that reverberated around the valley in the Nordpark area were the sign that there had been a fresh dump of snow. It was like music to his ears. An early-morning wake-up call that he loved.

Even the exposed walk along the mountain ridge to the Karrine was invigorating at this time of day. From here, the highest point of the mountain, he could ski to the Seegrube mid-station, one third of the way down the mountain, then on down one of the lengthy red runs through the trees back down to the Hungerburg area. It was his idea of heaven. And Samantha was trying to spoil it for him.

Skiing was the best part of the day. He enjoyed the solitude of the slopes. On the ski slopes he could forget about everything. As a child it had been a source of pure enjoyment. As an adult, it had brought back memories of happier times. The last few runs had been different. It had been like transporting himself into another world. One where his head wasn't pickled with thoughts of injections, doses, sugar levels and a whole host of other things he really didn't have the energy to think about right now. Swooshing down the clean white slopes could do that for him—lift the dark pressing cloud from his head and shoulders.

He had no idea where Samantha was. And he couldn't help but feel irritated. He couldn't shake the black mood that was circling around him. What did diabetes have to do with skiing? He hated anything interfering with his skiing. The fact that it was even on his mind as he was flying down the slopes grated. Nearly as much as last night's memory of a pair of bright blue eyes and a curved behind in a pair of denims that hugged in all the right places. And if he even gave a thought to the flash of bare breasts this morning he'd be done for.

This place was his haven. There was an invisibility to being on the slopes. With his hat and ski goggles on it was virtually impossible for anyone to recognise him. That was part of the reason he loved being around here so much. He didn't want anything to affect that. Checking blood sugars on a mountainside? It just didn't seem practical, no matter what his nurse might think.

He'd tried a little gentle flirting with Samantha last night. He hadn't been able to help it. It had been a natural reaction to being around a gorgeous woman. And Samantha Lewis was definitely in the gorgeous category—she was wasted being a nurse.

For a few minutes she'd almost flirted back. He liked it that she had a cheeky side. He'd spent too long around females who had no idea how to laugh at themselves and with those around them.

A bump on the slopes brought his attention back to the here and now. He bent a little lower, curving into the turns on the piste. He could hear the swish of a snowboard close behind him and see another few people at the bottom of the slope. Within the next hour the ski runs would start to get busy. Nordpark was a little unusual, ideal for beginners or extreme skiers, with very little for intermediate ones. He couldn't even guess what stage Samantha was at. But from the expression on her face last night she'd looked shocked at the mere mention of skiing.

She shouldn't be. He'd stipulated in his request for the perfect nurse that he needed someone who was able to accompany him on the slopes.

There she was. In his brain again. Where was this coming from?

He slowed, sweeping to a halt at the bottom of the run. His heart was pounding in his ears, the skin on his cheeks smarting from the cold air. The Seegrube mid-station was a little busier, even though it was still before eight.

The smell of breakfast wafted out to meet him as he stood for a few seconds on the terrace overlooking the valley. Mornings were gorgeous, but it was also beautiful up here in the early evening in the dimming light, with views from the restaurant all over the valley down to Innsbruck. Maybe he would bring her up here later.

And then he spotted it. The bright blue jacket and matching hat emerging from one of the cable cars. He was just about to walk over to one of the red runs and carry on down the slopes, but he could see her head darting around, looking everywhere to see if she could spot him. Where were her skis? He was getting a bad feeling about this. Could they still be in the cable car? This woman was beginning to exasperate him.

He unclipped his boots, and carried his skis and poles over towards her. But Samantha had stopped looking for him. She was too busy staring down the valley at the view. The cable-car building exited onto a terrace with spectacular views, and most people who came off the cable car came to an automatic halt as the sight took their breath away.

He could see the look of awe across her face, almost visible beneath her scowl. There was a little surge of pride in his chest. It seemed important that she like the surrounding area just as much as he did. They were nineteen hundred feet up here and the whole of Innsbruck was laid out beneath them like a miniature toy village. At the bottom of the mountain people moved around like ants, queuing for the cable cars, with some flashes of intermittent colour as skiers and snowboarders wound their way down the slopes.

He put his skis and poles over in a corner and walked up behind her. 'See something you like?'

She jumped and turned around, her nose almost brushing against his ski jacket. She lifted her head and frowned. She didn't look happy at all. 'Where on earth have you been, Mitchell? I told you I'd meet you here. I've been up and down on that cable car twice.' The tone of her voice was like that of a schoolteacher he'd had years ago. He hadn't liked her.

It was amazing how this woman could make him mad within a few seconds.

'Meeting up was your idea, not mine. And I never agreed to anything.'

She folded her arms across her chest. 'Do you know what, Mitchell? You seem to be forgetting that—like it or not—I'm your nurse.' She pointed to her chest. 'You are under *my* care. You might be used to being the boss, but things have changed.'

It was amazing, the talent she had to really rile him and make his blood fizz with pure anger in his veins.

'Who do you think you are? You aren't in charge of me. *I'm* employing you, remember?'

She shook her head. 'You might be footing the bill but until you've got this condition under control, you have to do what I say.'

'I don't have to do anything,' he spat back, making a few people near them turn around.

'Look, buddy, I'm the one that makes the decision about whether you're fit to do your tour or not. And not following my instructions? That isn't going to win you any prizes with me.'

He leaned forward, growling at her, 'I'm not your buddy.' It was the only coherent thing he could say right now. All meaningful arguments and sarcastic comments had sprinted from his brain in a fit of anger.

She sighed and rolled her eyes and he realised how pathetic he must be sounding. This woman made him feel like a naughty teenager. It had been a *long* time since someone had made him feel like that. He almost laughed out loud. No matter how much she was driving him crazy, she had a real spark about her. It was obvious she genuinely didn't care who he was. There was no way she was taking orders from him.

It was refreshing. He'd spent the last few years with everyone around him jumping to do his bidding. It was amazing what money could buy you.

She pointed over her shoulder towards the restaurant. 'I'm sincerely hoping that this snarkiness of yours is a symptom of hypo and not a personality trait. Because if it is...' she lifted her eyebrows '...*buddy*, you and I are about to board a roller-coaster. Now, let's eat, I'm starving. Some of us didn't get to eat breakfast this morning.'

And she didn't wait. She stalked off in front of him and into the canteen.

When was the last time that had happened? He shook his head and followed her, trying not to look at her butt in those jeans.

They walked through the glass doors and he was quickly assaulted by the familiar smell of roasting coffee beans, bacon and sweet pastries. Breakfast at the restaurant catered for all tastes.

He took a deep breath. If he played his cards right, he could get this over and done with in quick time. Then he might actually be able to hit the slopes again, and hopefully shake her off for the afternoon. He had things to do. It was time for the charm offensive—even if he didn't really mean it. He held out his hands and spun around. 'So, Sam, what do you fancy?'

She blushed. Instantly. The colour flooded into her cheeks. It was good for her. Out in the cold her skin had been even paler than before—this way she had colour about her.

The heat in her cheeks was matched by the rush of blood around his body. He'd been joking, of course he had. But, from the looks it, the thought of Mitchell as anything other than a patient had at least crossed her mind. That was good enough for him.

She hesitated. 'We really should sit somewhere and check your blood sugar. That's why I'm here. To make sure you don't run into any problems on the mountain.' Was she saying this out loud for his benefit or for hers?

'And how do you expect to do that in those?' He pointed at her flat rubber-soled boots, before looking around again. 'Where are your skis anyway?'

'Let's do this first.' She grabbed a tray and headed along the short line in the restaurant and he followed reluctantly. His stomach gave a growl. He was feeling hungry again, even though he'd had breakfast this morning. Then he remembered something else. The look on her face last night when he'd mentioned skiing. He'd assumed she just hadn't welcomed the early start. But now it was adding up to something else entirely.

There could be an opportunity to take Ms Bossy Boots down a peg or two. This could actually be fun.

Just then a group of boisterous boarders came flooding through the glass doors. It was obvious they were on the adrenaline high of just having finished a run. There were no manners, no decorum, it was almost like a bull stampede. Three of them jostled and knocked into Sam, all of them talking at the tops of their voices and not even noticing what they'd done.

She teetered then toppled, her face heading directly for the floor.

'Hey! Watch out!' He made a grab for Sam's arm, catching her just before she made contact with the floor. 'What do you think you're doing? You ignorant little gits.' He stood Sam back on her feet and turned to the nearest guy, who had an indignant look on his face, and gave him a shove that sent him flying into his pack of friends. 'How do you like it?'

He could feel the blood pumping through him, his temper flaring easily and his fingers clenching into fists. 'Who's next?'

The guys looked at one another, obviously contemplating whether to take him up on his offer or not. But Sam positioned herself between them all.

'Mitchell, stop it. I'm fine. Don't cause a scene.'

He was barely listening, still focused on the group of guys. 'I don't care about causing a scene. I care about people treating you as if you're not even there.'

One of the guys straightened himself and for a second it looked as if he was going to take Mitchell up on his offer. Instead, he offered a mumbled apology to Sam for knocking her over and moved away.

Just as quickly as the flare-up had started, it was snuffed out. Sam was still standing in front of him, eyes wide and slightly horrified.

He swallowed. Should he be embarrassed? Because he wasn't, not at all.

'Where were we?' He was starting to feel a little calmer.

'Breakfast,' she muttered, picking up her tray and pushing it along the line.

He picked up some wholegrain bread and put it in the nearby toaster, grabbing a handful of low-fat spread. He watched as she hesitated over the cheese and ham then selected a croissant with some butter and jam. They reached the part where the local barista was standing. *'Sacher melange.'* He nodded.

'What's that?' Sam asked as she pulled her woolly hat from her head, releasing her curls. Pretty as a picture. She was obviously calming down a little with him now. Trying to get things back onto an even keel.

'It's hot black coffee, foamed milk, topped with whipped cream. Want some?'

She sighed. 'We really need to talk about your dietary choices, Mr Brody.' She raised her eyebrows. 'And a few other things.'

'Forget it. The wholemeal toast cancels everything else out.' He folded his arms. 'And you don't get to advise on anything other than the diabetes.'

'Is that the way you work?'

'That's exactly the way I work.' He took his steaming cup from the server. '*Danke schoen*. What do you want?'

'I want a patient who'll take responsibility for his disease and be a grown-up about it.' The words were like a sucker punch. Just when he thought they might start being civil to each other she was reminding him exactly why she was there. He almost bit his lip to stop himself saying exactly what he wanted. 'Hey.' He shrugged. 'Don't hold back.'

She had no idea the impact all this was having on him.

When he'd started to feel unwell, all he'd been able to focus on had been the fatigue and weight loss. He'd convinced himself that he was going to be diagnosed with the same condition his brother had as a child—acute lymphoblastic leukaemia. He'd ignored the raging thirst and crazy appetite. He'd ignored the fact he didn't have obvious bruising. He'd only focused on the familiar. And it had filled him with fear and dread.

It had also stopped him from visiting the doctor until very late.

Diabetes should have been a diagnosis that filled him with relief. But for some strange reason it just didn't.

The thought that this disease—this…condition—had caused him to lose part of his evening was more than a little disturbing. His brain had been on overdrive in the early hours while he'd imagined other potential situations and their outcomes if something like that happened again.

He was no angel. The press he'd had was testament to that. But whatever he'd done in the past—and all the related consequences—had been outcomes of his actions. Things he'd *chosen* to do. Sure, on occasion there might have been a little alcohol or bad temper involved, but that didn't matter. He'd still been able to make a decision.

Last night had been nothing like that. Last night was a few fuzzy memories then a big black gaping hole. The thought of not being in control was playing nearly as much havoc with his senses as being around his new nurse.

She was talking about being a grown-up. Right now he wanted to play nursery games. Right now he wanted to stick his head in the sand and pretend he was an ostrich.

He had responsibilities she knew nothing about.

He glanced sideways. A small smile had started to creep across her face. She'd obviously realised he was ignoring her barbed comment.

Her stomach rumbled loudly and she laughed, squinting up at the menu on the wall written in German. She shrugged. 'Well, it's all double Dutch to me. I'll have the hot chocolate, thanks.'

She really was cute when she smiled. He was trying to see a way forward. Maybe he should try and win her around with his charm? The thought started to play around in his brain. He smiled, his eyebrows raised. 'With whipped cream?'

'Is there any other way?'

He grinned. 'Why, Ms Lewis, I think we need to discuss your dietary choices too.' He decided to move in for the kill. 'Have you ever been to Innsbruck before?'

'I've never been to Austria before. What kind of things are there to see around here?' She waved her hand around and laughed. 'Apart from the obvious.'

'There's loads to do around here. There's a zoo at the foot of the mountain. Did you see it? It's the highest zoo in Europe. And Christmas is really the best time of year to be here. There's a gorgeous Christmas tree in front of the Golden Roof, with a Christmas market in the surrounding square.' He couldn't hide the affection in his voice for the place that he loved. It was a whole lot easier to talk about this place than anything else.

She turned to face him again. 'A golden roof? On a house?'

'I'll take you there later. I'll explain then.'

She looked down through the glass and pointed at the houses on the edges of the city. 'I love the coloured houses. They look like sweeties. And I love the style of all the buildings. It's so atmospheric here.' She looked over in the other direction and pointed at the tall, distant silver and blue glass structure. 'And what's that? It's like something from the space age. It's like being in two different time zones here.'

'Ah, that's Bergisel, the ski jump. It was built in 2002. There are lots of ski and snowboarding competitions held there.' He gave her a wink. 'They've even got a panoramic restaurant too.' He glanced over his shoulder. 'But I prefer this one.'

There it was again. That little flicker of something. He just didn't know what.

She wasn't girlfriend material. She was his nurse. He just couldn't quite equate this girl with a twinkle in her eye to the Dragon Lady in the hospital. It was hard for him to put people into boxes—that they should be just one thing.

She was watching a snowboarder moving more quickly than a speeding car, weaving his way down the mountain with skill and expertise. But she was frowning. He could almost picture her brain computing all the possible injuries. There was no love for the sport on her face.

'Do you board?' he asked.

'Not in this lifetime,' she muttered, and gave a little shudder. She hadn't even realised she'd answered.

His smile grew wider. He'd bet if he put Samantha Lewis on a snowboard or pair of skis she'd spend most of her time face-planting in the snow. It wasn't an ideal situation, but for the moment he was inclined to go with the flow. It could be fun.

He settled the bill while they waited for her order then carried the tray over to a nearby table that looked out over the spectacular view. 'There's a terrace outside. It's still a little cold right now, but around lunchtime lots of people will be sitting out there, eating their sandwiches.'

Someone walked past with a huge pile of pastries and chocolate cake on their tray. Samantha shook her head, shuddered and squeezed her eyes closed. 'It's eight in the morning. How can they eat those?'

The smell of hot chocolate was drifting all around her and as she bent over the steam tickled her nose. She pulled out the monitor from her pocket and put it on the table.

'Check your blood glucose before you start eating.'

He stared at it on the table between them—like a stand-off. It only took one deep breath to make up his mind. One sharp inhalation of the crisp new snow and the fresh smell of the pine and larch trees surrounding the area made him realise he wanted this over and done with.

'Bossy boots.'

'Says the man who had a monster-sized temper tantrum first thing this morning, and then again here.' She leaned back in her chair. 'Don't push me, Mitchell. Last time I saw one of those I was dealing with a three-year-old.'

He gave her a wry smile. 'Who won?'

'You have to ask?'

'I guess not.'

Yip. The rock star was going to be a monster-sized problem. And in a way it annoyed the life out of her. She hadn't been joking when she'd called him on his temper tantrum. How come it seemed okay to tell kids when behaviour was inappropriate but not adults? Particularly adults who were paying your giant wage.

A wave of emotions started simmering to the surface. She'd phoned her mum before she'd come up the mountain this morning. She'd sounded great—so happy with the nursing-home staff and the care she was receiving. It was just the reminder she needed as to why she was doing this.

The home before had been awful. The staff hadn't been bad, there just hadn't been enough of them, meaning the standard of care had been low. Hell would freeze over before she let her mother go back there.

As for Mitch? She probably wasn't handling him as well as she could, but at least for now he was doing as he was told.

It took him less than thirty seconds to check his blood sugar. Five. His stomach grumbled again. 'I'd planned on going back down the piste and finishing that run. I would have come back for something to eat then.'

She pulled her gloves off and reached across the table, her hand touching his. It surprised her how warm his skin was. 'You need to eat. Any lower than that and you would start to hypo again. Skiing obviously burns off a lot of energy. Finishing the run and then getting food might have been too late.' She let her words hang in the air as he buttered his toast and started eating.

His eyes were fixed on something on the horizon now and she could tell he was in a bad mood. But that was too bad. Mitchell needed her there. He needed constant reminders that he couldn't just forget about his diabetes. There was no reason that he couldn't continue to ski. He would just have to make sure he had things under control.

His gloves and hat were sitting on the chair next to him, his hair sticking up in every direction but the right one.

There was something vaguely familiar about all this. 'Don't you advertise hair products?' she said as she took a sip of the hot chocolate. Hmm. 'Ooh, this is fantastic. It definitely hits the spot.'

He ran his fingers through his mussed-up hair. 'Yip, and I have about a million dollars' worth of products in my garage in LA. Here? I have nothing. Haven't you heard grunge is in?'

She laughed. His eyes met hers again. There was something else there. A flicker of something she hadn't seen before. Worry. Stress. Or maybe the distracted look was just how he was before he started to hypo.

She pushed his coffee towards him. 'Drink this and finish your toast.' And to her surprise, he did. The coffee seemed to settle him. The cream and milk, along with the wholemeal toast, would help bring his blood-glucose levels up in a steady manner. She spread the jam and butter on her croissant and consumed it along with her hot chocolate. 'If I do this every day, I'll put on twenty pounds,' she sighed.

His brown eyes fixed on hers. A little twinkle appeared. 'Don't worry, Samantha. You'll work off all those calories again with your skiing.'

It was the way he'd said it. The tone and intonation of his voice. It was almost as if he was taunting her. Almost as if he knew.

'I didn't bring skis,' she said quickly. 'No one mentioned anything about skiing when I took the job.'

'Even though it was a condition for my nurse?'

'Really? Yikes.'

He reached over and gave her hand a squeeze. 'Well, don't worry. I'll hire you a set up here. That's no problem at all. Now, which piste would you like to go down first? You've never been here before, and there isn't much for intermediate skiers. Would you like me to shadow you down?' He leaned forward. 'Look at it out there. All that perfect powder. Think about the feel of the air rushing past those curls of yours.' He reached over and brushed his hand to the side of them.

The rat bag. He definitely knew.

She fixed him with a hard stare as she took another sip of her hot chocolate then held up the glass towards him and used her best sarcastic tone. 'You know, you're spoiling this for me.'

'How's that?'

'You know I can't ski. Why don't you just give it up?'

'You can't ski?' She couldn't help but laugh at the mock horror on his face. 'But everyone can ski, Samantha.'

She rolled her eyes. 'Maybe if you have a billionaire chalet in a ski resort. The rest of us chumps just go on a very bad ski trip with the school and vow never to put on a pair of skis again.' She leaned forward to emphasise her last word. 'Ever.'

'Come on, Samantha, it's fun. I'll get someone to teach you. Think of the feel of the wind in your hair and the air rushing past your cheeks. Come to think of it, have you got sunscreen and lip balm on?'

She shook her head. He reached into the inside pocket of his jacket and tossed her a small tube. 'Total sunblock. Put it all over your face, your ears and the back of your neck. You're almost as white as the snow, you'll burn in an instant.'

She examined it in her hands, her nose wrinkled. 'See? That's what's wrong here. I shouldn't need to think about this kind of stuff. All I should be worrying about is if you're going to fall off this mountain or not.' She raised her hands. 'While there's no denying the view is spectacular, why couldn't you have had a hideaway on some mysterious Caribbean island? I know how to swim. I know how to sunbathe. I might even have agreed to go jet-skiing with you.

And there I would have known to wear sunscreen when I was out at seven in the morning.'

He took a sip of his coffee and shook his head. 'How did you get this job, Samantha?'

For a second she felt offended. 'What do you mean?'

'I mean, I deliberately specified that I needed someone who could ski and not only that but they could extreme ski and accompany me on the slopes.'

'You did?' She was shocked. Not once had Trish mentioned the skiing part. But then again she'd been desperate to find someone—anyone—to take the job. And she had been desperate for the money.

He nodded solemnly. 'I did.' He was teasing her again.

'Well, I hate to break it to you, Mitchell, but extreme skiing, diabetic nurse specialists, on a few hours' notice, over Christmas and New Year—well, they seem to be in short supply. After all, I had to fight off at least a thousand others to get here.' She started laughing at him. 'Do you really think you can buy whatever you want?'

'Face it, Sam. Everything's for sale—and everybody. Tell me, why exactly are you working over Christmas and New Year? Don't you have a regular job? Isn't there anyone you want to spend Christmas and New Year with?' he countered. Smart guy. Nosey too.

She could easily take umbrage at those words. 'I do have a regular job. One that I changed just recently and it means I get Christmas and New Year off. I worked last year at this time, and at Easter. Agency work at this time of year pays well.' She stopped there. No need to say any more. He knew exactly how much he was paying for her services. She was annoyed by his comment that everybody was for sale but didn't really feel in a position to argue with him about it, given the circumstances.

But he wasn't about to stop. 'So, is money an issue for you, Sam?'

She bristled at his words. Cheeky git. 'Is money an issue for you, Mitchell?'

His eyes immediately fixed on the horizon. 'You just never know,' he murmured.

She shifted in her chair. Her comeback had been more than a little tetchy. She hadn't really meant to sound like that. After all, this job was going to save her money problems for the next six months. And she wasn't too sure about his response. Surely the last thing a man like Mitchell Brody would have was money problems.

She shrugged. Time to cover her foot-in-mouth disease. 'I don't know what the big deal is about having a nurse that can ski. As long as I'm around the slopes and can keep an eye on you it shouldn't be a problem. I quite liked the ride up in the cable car. I'm happy to keep doing that.'

'But what if I have a hypo attack while I'm skiing?'

She took a deep breath. 'You'll check your blood sugar before you start. If it's low, you'll eat something and wait until it comes back up before you get going. Face it, Mitchell, whether you like it or not, you're going to have to meet me at regular intervals.'

He baulked then groaned and she raised her eyebrows, trying not to feel insulted. 'The medical science isn't there to change this right now. Don't fight me on this. For once in your life be sensible.'

His expression changed. The cheeky glint in his eyes was back. 'You think I'm not sensible?'

She looked out over the snow at the busying slopes as she stirred the contents of her mug. 'I'm just saying that I'm not the one who got caught on a rooftop in New York, in the middle of a snowstorm, naked.'

He went to interrupt but she lifted her hand. 'And I'm not the one who decided the best way to pick a new car was to buy one in every colour.'

He sat back. 'Oh, yeah, that.' He shrugged his shoulders. 'The first one…I'm not admitting to. The second? Well, maybe…but not *every* colour. I definitely didn't get the yellow.'

'The yellow? Why not? I would have thought that matched your sunny personality?'

He threw back his head and laughed. 'Oh, snarky Samantha. I like it. Can I see more, please?'

She stood up. 'There's lot's more where that comes from. Now, come on. I take it you want to ski down? I can catch the cable car back down and meet you there. I can do this all day.'

He shook his head. 'Actually, I planned on finishing after my third run. I come early so I can ski before the slopes get busy. I have other things to do.'

'Like what?' She was feeling hopeful. Maybe they would go into Innsbruck and see a little of the city.

Something flickered across his eyes. It looked like he was about to say something then the shutters slammed down and he stood up.

'Look, Sam, I've done what you asked. I'll finish my ski run and meet you once more at the bottom of the mountain. After that—that's it. I don't need to tell you every minute of my day. You work for me, remember?'

He picked up his hat and gloves and stalked away, leaving Sam stunned.

What on earth had just happened there?

CHAPTER FOUR

FOR THE FOURTH day in a row, Mitchell failed to meet her when he should have.

She was ready to erupt. It was like dealing with a child, not an adult, and she was getting sick to death of it.

She'd never met a rock star before, but she'd worked with enough kids to understand when someone wasn't taking things seriously. When someone was running scared.

She stepped out of the cable car. It was five o'clock in the evening. For the fourth day in a row, Mitch had skied the slopes in the morning and disappeared without a backward glance in the afternoon. It was driving her crazy.

Had he really no respect for her and the job she was doing?

She wandered around the Seegrube station, trying to spot his red jacket. She'd almost given up hope when she heard his laugh. His deep, hearty laugh.

She rounded the corner to the terrace. She really hadn't expected to find him here, but as time had marched on she hadn't really known where else to look.

And there he was. Not a blooming care in the world. Laughing and drinking with a group of guys she'd never seen before.

She blinked. Drinking. Drinking *beer*.

The red mist started to descend around her. She'd reached her limit with this guy.

She walked straight through the middle of the drinking buddies. 'Mitch?'

A silence fell over the group, quickly followed by a snigger then a low whistle.

Samantha ignored them all. 'You were supposed to meet me back at the house at four.'

Four days in a row. Four days in a row she'd sat and stared at four walls in his luxury chalet while he'd been who-knew-where. It made her mad. It made her seethe.

She might have agreed to work over Christmas but that didn't mean she didn't miss her family—didn't miss her mum. At least for the last two years she'd always felt useful. She'd been kept busy with Daniel and his family and that had stopped her missing her mum too much. But this? This wasn't working for her at all. Her patience had finally run out. It didn't matter how much she needed the money right now, being treated like crap and having her professional advice ignored was the last straw.

He looked more than a little stunned. Embarrassed by her. 'Give it a rest, Samantha,' he murmured, trying to appear casual.

'Snarky girlfriend,' came the murmur behind her.

She tilted her chin. 'No, Mitchell. I won't give it a rest. We had a meeting. That's the fourth day in a row you've blown me off. It's about time you started to take this seriously.' She pointed at the bottle in his hand. 'Beer, Mitchell? Really?' She paused, conscious of the audience around them. She glared at him. 'You and I need to talk. Now.'

Mitch felt the blood rush into his cheeks. He wasn't embarrassed—well, yes, actually, he was. But the rush of blood was due to the fury building in his chest.

He stood up and grabbed hold of Samantha's wrist and pulled her behind him. He could hear the yelps and cat calls from the snowboarding guys. The shouts of 'Being whipped' and 'Under the thumb'.

He walked quickly, rounding the corner away from the crowds, away from the bustle of people exiting the cable cars, and pulled her up next to him.

'Don't you ever do that to me again!'

She didn't even flinch. 'Likewise.'

'What's that supposed to mean?' All he wanted was a bit of peace. A bit of privacy. These few weeks were supposed to be his holiday. His chance to kick back and relax before the tour. If he wanted to have a beer with a few friends, then that's exactly what he would do. And he certainly didn't need Samantha Lewis's permission for that.

'I'm sick of this. It's about time you started to take this seriously. I can't help you get your diabetes under control if you don't follow my instructions. These first few weeks are vital. This is the time we need to iron out any problems.'

She was serious. Her pretty face was marred by a frown. And she had a weary look in her eyes. But he was too angry to care.

'Right now my only problem is you.'

'Then I'll say it again. Likewise. This isn't working for me, Mitch. I'm ready to pack up and go home and spend Christmas with my mum. Why waste my time here? Why waste my time on you? You don't deserve it. You don't care. So why should I?' She looked him up and down. 'I'm not here because I like you, Mitch. I'm not here because I'm a fan. I'm here because I'm paid to be.'

He got it that she was mad. He just didn't expect her to slam dunk him like that. Nothing like getting to the point.

'Who are you to tell me I don't care? Of course I care. I care about my tour. I need to be well to go on tour. That's why you're here, Sam. To make sure I'm fit enough to do the tour. But I don't need to report in to you every second of the day. I'm entitled to a private life of my own. And I certainly don't need you to babysit me.'

She sighed and shook her head. 'Actually, you do. That's exactly what I'm being paid for right now.' She folded her arms and stared off into the distance. 'That's it, Mitch. I can't say you're fit for your tour. I don't think you're taking this seriously at all. It would compromise my professional competency if I said you were fit when you clearly aren't.'

She looked him squarely in the eye. 'I won't do it. You might want to put your health at risk, but the nurse in me won't allow that to happen. You won't tell me where you're going or what you're doing. I can't help you monitor your levels or plan your meals or insulin doses. I'm not prepared to keep banging my head against a brick wall.' She lifted her hands. 'You just don't get it. I don't actually *care* what you're doing or who you're doing it with. I just need to know. I need you to work with me. I need *you* to care.'

The penny dropped like a hammer to the head. She thought he was sneaking away every afternoon for some secret rendezvous with a lady. He tried not to smile as he imagined how she thought he was expending his energy.

And as much as he hated to admit it, she had him. He needed her. He needed her to sign him off as fit for this tour.

He let out a sigh of exasperation. He hated everything about this. He had never explained himself to anyone. Starting now, at this stage in his life, was unthinkable.

'I'm done, Brody. Book me on the next flight home.' Her voice was subdued, almost whispered. She was staring out over the landscape with those killer blue eyes and a resigned look on her face. He'd pushed her too far.

Samantha wasn't like every other employee. He couldn't push her around like he had others.

Something inside him cracked.

If she told the insurers he wasn't adhering to his treatment plan, his whole tour would go up in smoke. A wave of panic started to wash over him. He hadn't really believed it was a possibility. For some strange reason, he'd just assumed she wouldn't do that.

Obviously not. It was a harsh reality check.

It was time to try and salvage what he could—to stop her leaving on the next available plane.

He took a deep breath. 'Sam, I'm going to tell you something that hardly anyone on this planet knows.'

Her brow furrowed. She recognised the sincerity in his voice, and since it was something she hadn't heard much, she obviously took it seriously. 'Okay,' she said slowly.

He put his hands on her shoulders and spun her round to look out over the view below. 'See that building with the green roof, off to the left?'

She squinted as the sun was in her eyes. 'Yeah, I think so. The one that sits by itself? What is that?'

'It's the children's hospital. That's where I spend most of my afternoons.'

He heard her sharp intake of breath. She spun back round, concern written all over her face. 'What haven't you been telling me? You have a sick kid? A relative?' Her voice trembled as she spoke. 'Why do you spend so much time at the children's hospital, Mitch?'

It was time to put everything out there. He had to stop her leaving. 'Because that's where I spent most of my childhood.'

CHAPTER FIVE

IT WAS LIKE being home. This was one of the few places on the planet that Mitchell Brody felt entirely relaxed, entirely himself.

As soon as they crossed the threshold of the children's hospital it was like being in another world. The temperature was different, the mood was different—even the lighting was different. Lots of these kids were pale to the point of almost being blue and the warm-coloured lighting seemed to lessen the severity of their appearance. Making them look not quite so unwell.

More importantly, around Christmastime the staff always bent over backwards to make the whole place something special. There was a huge Christmas tree at the entrance, another at the end of the corridor, and another in the kids' playroom, each decorated in a different colour. A whole variety of kids' paintings showing Santa and reindeers and multicoloured presents decorated the walls. Even the kids who were in isolation—at risk of any kind of infection—had fibreoptic trees outside their windows, so the changing lights would be reflected back inside their rooms.

He gave a quick hug to the nurse in charge. 'Lisa, this is my friend Samantha Lewis. She's here to visit with me today.'

Lisa's smile reached from one ear to the other. She was

always glad to see him. There were never any airs or graces here. The truth was if he tried to order someone around here he'd get a swift kick to the butt. And he liked it. It was exactly how it should be.

Lisa gave Samantha an interested nod. He'd never brought anyone with him before, apart from Dave, of course. But he was careful not to introduce Samantha as a nurse. He didn't want to give anything away. He particularly didn't want to alert any of the staff at the children's hospital to his health issues. No way. He didn't want them to think that anything would get in the way of him funding the new build.

Lisa checked some notes. 'Okay, Rooms 4 and 5 are out of bounds.' It was the quickest glance that spoke volumes. The children in those rooms must be at the end of their lives. The muscles in his chest tightened. He'd been there. There had been a few times that they'd thought his brother might not make it. But they'd all been lucky. He was still here.

But lots of other families didn't get the miracle that they had. Even though cancer was better diagnosed and treatments were better targeted some kids were just too sick to get better. And this children's hospital didn't just look after children with cancer. It looked after children with a whole range of conditions that could be terminal. No child and their family would ever be turned away from St Jude's Children's Hospital.

'No problem. Is there anywhere you want me to spend time?'

She smiled and gave him a nod. 'You know there is. Luke Reynolds in Room 3 would love a visit. Brian Flannigan, the teenager in Room 14 would love to play guitar with you, and Lindsay Davenport, the twelve-year-old in Room 17, wants some Hollywood gossip.' She raised her eyebrows. 'She particularly wants to know if Reid Kerr from your band is secretly dating a supermodel.'

'Aha.' He couldn't help but smile. The kids here were great. Most of them were constantly surrounded by friends and family, but sometimes it helped to have another face in the mix.

Lisa turned to Samantha. 'How are you with babies?'

Her eyes widened and she looked a little shocked. To be honest, he was breathing a huge sigh of relief that she'd actually agreed to stay at all. He should have warned her that it was all hands on deck in here. But she was a nurse, he was sure she could cope.

'I deal mostly with teenagers...' she nodded her head slowly '...but I'm sure I can help out with a baby. What can I do for you?' She was already unzipping her jacket, ready to get to work.

'We've got a young mum whose four-year-old has leukaemia. She's got a new baby too, who has a real dose of colic.' She smiled sympathetically. 'It might be a bit on your ears, but would you mind giving mum some respite so she can spend time with her son?'

Samantha nodded her head and pushed up her sleeves. 'No problem. I can pace the floors with a colicky baby. Which room?'

Lisa pointed down the corridor. 'Room 8. Mum will know I've sent you. There's a quiet room at the bottom of the corridor that no one else is using. It's got some music and nice lighting, and some rocking chairs. You could try in there if you like.'

Sam put her arm on Mitch's arm. 'Okay, I'll see you in a little while. Come and find me if you need me.'

She was being serious. She'd obviously picked up on the fact he hadn't mentioned who she was but was still trying to make sure he understood why she was doing this.

He was still a little worried she hadn't made up her mind about staying yet.

She walked down the corridor and he couldn't help but admire her curves in her figure-hugging jeans. Lisa followed his gaze and folded her arms across her chest. 'Well, Mitchell, who is that?'

There was amusement in her voice and a gleam in her eyes. He met her grin head on. 'I have no idea what you mean.'

Lisa had worked here for three years. She was fantastic with the kids, mainly because she was good at reading people. And she was using all her professional skills on him right now. 'I like her,' she said approvingly. 'She didn't hesitate to help. I'm just surprised to finally meet one of your friends.' She gave him a knowing nod and emphasised the final word.

'It's not like that,' he said quickly. Too quickly. Because it just made her grin even wider.

She copied Sam's movements and tapped his arm as she walked past. 'Not yet it's not. But give it time...'

She grabbed an apron, gloves and mask and walked off to one of the other rooms. Darn it. She could read him too well. It was almost as if she could see all the pictures that were being conjured up in his mind. And one thing was for sure—they definitely couldn't be shared.

He pushed all thoughts from his mind. He loved this place but, for the first time, being here made him feel a little uncomfortable. Maybe it was the unspoken looks in all the staff's eyes. The expectation that he was about to make things so much better for them.

And he would. No matter how sick he was, or what else was going on in his life. He couldn't let anything get in the way of this tour and the money he would earn for the children's hospital. Never mind what Samantha Lewis's cute behind looked like in those jeans. She was only interested in his blood-sugar levels. Not his hormone levels.

He checked the board again and made his way towards Luke Reynolds's room. The little guy had an insatiable urge to play board games. He was only six but Risk was his favourite and he was ruthless. A few weeks ago he'd been in isolation because his blood count had been so low. It was good that he was finally picking up a little.

Spending some time with Luke was a sure-fire guarantee that he could put everything else out of his mind. His tour. His disease. His nurse.

Samantha's ears were ringing. Ninety minutes. That's how long little Rose had screamed for, drawing her legs up in pain from the colic. It was no wonder her mum needed a break to spend time with her already exhausted four-year-old.

Sam had done everything she could think of—rocking, massaging, walking. But colic was hit or miss. Sometimes you just had to hold the little one and offer some comfort.

Finally Rose was exhausted and snuggled against Sam's pink woolly jumper. Was that a snore? She was in the rocking chair now; soothing music was playing in the background and there were interchanging coloured lights in the corners of the room. Any more of this and she would fall asleep herself.

She checked her watch. It really was time to find Mitchell and ask him to check his blood-glucose level again. It should be fine. They'd had lunch together before they'd got here and he'd eaten sensibly. She was just worried that his exercise from earlier could cause his glucose levels to dip a little later in the day.

Moving as silently as possible, she put Rose into her pram and walked her down the corridor towards her brother's room. She gave her mother a signal through the glass and left the pram outside.

She wasn't sure what room Mitchell would be in but strolled slowly along the corridor to see if she could hear his voice.

But it wasn't his voice that she heard. It was the sounds of a reverberating guitar filtering through the door. Lisa gave her a smile as she hurried past, nodding her head in the direction of the room. 'Soundproofed. Just as well!'

Samantha's hand hesitated at the door handle. Should she go in, or should she wait?

She was curious about Mitchell in this environment. He seemed to have left the rock persona at the door. This was all about the kids and there was something so nice about seeing that.

Lots of things about him were surprising her. With the exception of Dave and the cleaning service, he wasn't surrounded by 'people' doing his bidding. He didn't have an entourage. She hadn't even heard him mention his manager.

The house was gorgeous, and the furniture and equipment were miles out of her price range. But his stubborn streak and lack of acceptance of his condition were still a major headache. If he didn't start following the rules, this could all end in disaster.

Truth was, the most disturbing thing about Mitch was being at close quarters with him. The photo shoots and calendars didn't do the man justice. He had a way of looking at you that made you feel you were the only person in the room. On some occasions she had been, but the rest of the times?

It made her feel like a fool. It made her feel unfocused and unprofessional. She was here to do a job. That was all. In a few weeks' time she would be back in rainy London, working in a school in Brixton again.

The revelation about the hospital had been a bolt out of

the blue. She'd never heard a word in the press about any of this. But he had been quite clear that no one knew he helped out here—and it was to stay that way.

She turned the handle on the door. The noise almost blasted her backwards and she quickly stepped inside and closed the door behind her.

Neither male had noticed her, because both of them were on the bed, playing some kind of electric guitars and shaking their heads like mad rockers.

She recognised the tune—of course she did. It had been number one in numerous countries around the world for weeks.

But watching this kid, this teenager, rocking out with Mitch was something else entirely. Mitch might have been sick, but he looked a whole lot healthier than this young boy with no hair left on his head and skin so pale it was almost translucent. What was magnificent—what really pulled at her heartstrings—was the absolute energy and commitment the young boy had to the task at hand. He was having the time of his life.

The music built to a crescendo. The speed of their hands on the strings increasing, followed by a scream from each as they leapt off the bed towards her. They'd obviously done this before.

Before the last echoes of notes had even left the room they were high-fiving each other and laughing loudly.

'Fabulous, Brian, you get better every time.'

The young boy's eyes sparkled at the praise from his idol and Mitchell looked genuinely happy to be there. This wasn't a rock star doing something to help his image. No one even knew that he came here. It surprised her that one of the kids or their relatives hadn't spilled the beans to the press. But maybe his obvious pleasure at being here motivated them all to keep quiet. This place was a haven, very much like Mitchell's home.

If the press knew about his involvement the quiet and sanctity of this place would be destroyed in a heartbeat.

'I don't know why I'm getting better, my teacher's old enough to be my dad!' Brian's teenage bravado was coming through, but the look on his face and his trembling lips told Samantha that he was barely containing himself beneath the surface. Her nursing instincts kicked in straight away and she walked over then put her arm around his shoulders.

'Well, old teacher or not, that was the first time I've heard you and I thought you were fabulous.' She gave him a conspiratorial wink. 'In fact, I think you might even have been better than your teacher. You look tired after that. How about we find you something to drink and some cakes? I'm sure they'll have some around here.'

Mitchell gave her a little nod and she steered Brian out of the room and down the corridor to the TV room, where one of the staff was just setting out sodas and cookies. Once she was sure he was settled she went back to find Mitchell.

He was sitting at the nursing station with his feet on the desk, sprawled out across a chair, breathing heavily. It wasn't just Brian who was tired.

She pulled up a chair next to him as he opened one eye and looked at her. 'Did you bring me a cake, too?'

She shook her head. 'If you behave and check your blood sugar, I'll hunt you down a coffee and an apple.'

It was almost as if an unheard clock struck somewhere but doors started opening around them and kids and their parents all started filtering down to the TV room, where more food was being set out.

Mitch saw her curious expression and shrugged. 'Some of the kids can't eat around dinnertime. They like to have a constant supply of food around this place, and while most of it is healthy, they are pretty lenient with the kids.' He pulled his feet from the desk and leaned forward, resting his elbows on his knees. His voice had lowered, 'Sometimes, if they're midway through chemo, they just can't face regular food. At that point the staff will give them anything that they can stomach to get some calories in them. I once had to go out at midnight to try and track down a particular kind of candy bar.'

She smiled. There was no one around them now. It was just the two of them, alone.

She sat forward too, her hair cascading around her shoulders.

'Brian's got the same kind of leukaemia that my brother Shaun had—acute lymphoblastic leukaemia. That's why I spent a lot of time here as a kid.'

Her eyes widened and her stomach flipped over but he waved his hand. 'Don't ask. Not now. I'll tell you later.'

Of course. Things were starting to make sense. She'd wondered why he spent time here. Only someone who had firsthand experience would have such a good relationship with the staff. She just hadn't expected this. It was like a bolt from the blue.

But Mitch was focused again. He kept talking. 'Brian's not been so lucky. Even though it was caught early, his leukaemia's been really aggressive. Some days I come to visit and he can't even lift his head from the pillow. Days like this are good days.'

Her head was spinning but as he said the final words with a big sigh it made her realise he was still a little more out of breath than he cared to admit. The onset of his diabetes had implications for his health. With the skiing this morning, followed by more this afternoon, his body wasn't quite ready for all the physical exercise, but somehow she knew that asking Mitchell Brody to slow down would be pointless.

And a little part of her didn't want to. She didn't want to hide the person that Mitchell was, and would continue to be. Even though he was probably in recovery mode, it was important that she help him mould his diabetes to his life—within reason, of course. He had to be able to live normally and function on his own.

She looked up. Their heads were so close they could be touching, but Mitchell had his eyes closed. It could be fatigue, or it could be the emotion of what he'd just shared.

She couldn't think of him as a patient right now. Every instinct in her body wanted to comfort him and she did the most natural thing in the world for her. She reached out and touched him.

His hand was warm and soft, and as her palm brushed over the back of his hand he flipped it over and intertwined his fingers with hers. There were no sweaty palms here. There was just a whole host of tingles shooting straight up her arm.

He closed his fingers a little more. Locking their hands together. His eyes were still closed and his breathing was slowing. She was mesmerised by the rise and fall of his chest.

Suddenly his eyes opened, darker brown than ever, and fixed on her face. He leaned forward a little more and she felt her breath hitch in her throat. He rested his forehead against hers.

What am I doing? her brain was screaming in her ears. But she couldn't move—she couldn't pull her hand away from his. She didn't want to break this moment. No matter how many messages reverberated around her brain.

They stayed like that for more than a minute. Then his head lifted slightly and his eyelashes brushed against her forehead, before he dropped a gentle kiss on her head. His other hand came up and rested at the back of her hair. 'Thank you for coming with me today, Samantha.'

Words were stuck in her throat. Anything that came out right now would make her sound like a blundering idiot. This was crazy, but it felt special. She didn't feel like a teenage fan girl any more. She certainly didn't feel like his nurse. She felt something else entirely.

She stared down at their still intertwined hands. It was so much easier than looking up—if she did, they'd be nose to nose and she didn't even want to guess what could happen next.

She sucked a breath to steady her nerves and licked her, oh, so dry lips. 'Any time, Mitchell.' Her voice sounded so much steadier than she actually felt. She pulled back a little. There. That was better. Now she could look at him.

'I've liked it here today.' Her words were almost whispered. 'I've liked you here today.' Saying them out loud made her feel very vulnerable. 'I feel as if I understand you a little better now.' Was she saying that to quantify what she'd just said before? Her insides were instantly cringing, wishing she could pull those words back.

This time when he smiled at her it wasn't with his trademark rock-star smile. It wasn't the kind of confident smile he used, knowing he was one of the sexiest guys on the planet. This smile was totally different and it reached right up into his dark eyes.

He held her gaze. Her lungs were going to explode. *Please look away so I can breathe soon.* 'Me too,' he finally said, as he untangled his hand from her hair and stood up.

It was over. That little minute was gone. But he hadn't let go of her hand and he gave it a little tug. 'Let's go and join in the cake party.'

All her good intentions about healthy eating shot out of the window. 'Sure,' she said, as she wiped her other hand on her jeans and allowed him to lead her down the corridor towards the TV room.

What on earth was she doing?

CHAPTER SIX

MITCH STARED OUT at his view of the perfect snow. Today it wasn't perfect. Today it was blighted by little blue and red figures dotted around on the landscape in amongst the trees. On any other day he might have gone out and shouted that they were on private property. But right now he just didn't have the energy. Plus the fact he didn't seem to have a sensible thought in his head right now.

They'd come back from the children's hospital a few hours ago, the palm of his hand still burning from where he'd tangled it in her hair and held her hand. He wasn't quite sure what had happened between them.

Had anything really happened? He just knew he'd been inches away from devouring those perfect pink lips. For a few moments at the nurses' station they'd felt like the only two people in the world. Samantha hadn't been looking at him like his nurse. She hadn't been looking at him like some love-struck fan either. She'd been looking at him as if she finally got him. Finally got the kind of person that he was and what was important to him.

It was a connection. He just didn't know what to do about it.

Part of him felt that it was his fault. He'd never taken anyone to the children's hospital before. That part of his life was totally private. So why had he felt the urge to share it with Sam? He didn't understand himself.

Maybe it was because she'd held him to ransom this afternoon. She'd told him she was ready to quit and walk away.

He'd sat down an hour ago in his recliner chair to stare out at his private view. And that had been the last thing he remembered. This lack of energy and total physical exhaustion was driving him nuts. He'd always been the kind of guy who could be up early and stay awake easily to the small hours. He'd kind of assumed once he'd got a diagnosis and started his insulin that everything would just return to normal. But it was official. This diabetes was kicking his butt. Maybe it was interfering with his brain too?

He also had the biggest range of Christmas decorations in the world to put up. After Sam's remarks about missing out, he'd asked the company just to deliver the decorations and planned that he and Sam could put them up together. He wasn't quite sure why he'd done that—and he hadn't even told Sam yet. It would have been so much easier to let someone else do it, but Sam had seemed sad that day.

There was a quiet knock at the door. 'Mitchell, are you okay in there?' She peeked around the door and he pushed the recliner upright with a bang.

'Yeah, yeah. I'm fine.'

'Good. We need to talk.' She walked across the room and perched at the end of his sleigh-style bed. He gulped. Boy, oh, boy. He was trying not to admire her curves in the figure-hugging jeans or the way the blonde curls bobbed as she strode across the room. He was especially trying not to think about pushing her backwards onto that bed.

'We need to try something new. A little different.'

Wow. Where was this conversation about to go? He was all ears.

She reached her hand up and started twiddling with her

ear. 'We need to let you hypo in a controlled environment. We need to see what warning signs you have and if you can recognise them.'

'What?' He was standing now. Apart from the fact it was so not what he was expecting to hear, he didn't like the sound of this at all. 'Are you crazy? You've seen me hypo once—why do you need to see it again?'

She stood up and took a step closer. It seemed that their earlier interaction made her not so conscious of keeping him at arm's length. 'This isn't about what I've seen, Mitch. This is about you. It's all about you. And it's not crazy.' She folded her arms across her chest. 'A teenager or child who was newly diagnosed with insulin-dependent diabetes would never be allowed to go home until they'd hypoed in a controlled environment, preferably with both their parents there to recognise the signs and symptoms. It's part of the learning process about the condition.'

He wrinkled his nose. 'Well, I don't like the sound of it.' He waved his arm towards the window. 'Look at it out there. The sun's just about to go down. I was thinking we could go down into Innsbruck and have dinner somewhere. Doesn't that sound much more like a plan?'

He saw it. That fleeting moment of temptation that raced through her eyes. But she kept her resolve, stepping forward and touching the seam of his shirt at the front of his chest. Was this a persuasive tactic? Because he could tell her right now it would work.

'It does sound like a plan. But I'm in charge of planning, Mitch, not you. So we're going to do things my way. We'll do the hypo first, and if you feel up to it, we'll eat dinner later.'

He liked the way her voice had a little stern edge to it. He liked it even better that her eyes didn't look quite so distant as before.

'I'm not sure I want to do this. I lost two hours of my

life last time around.' The words were out before he had a chance to think about them. And he cringed. They made him sound weak. It was so not what he was.

But Samantha nodded her head slowly. 'I get that, Mitch, I do. I hate the feeling of not being in control. But this is important. This will ultimately let you be more in control. It will give you the chance to realise if something is going wrong and take corrective steps to stop you getting worse. Last time around wasn't a good example.' She hesitated for a second. 'Do you want to ask Dave to be here? It's important that he can recognise signs too.'

Mitch shook his head. 'No. Absolutely not. Dave can't handle this kind of stuff. If this is going to happen, it's just you...' he met her gaze '...and me.'

'You and me.' She repeated the phrase, holding his gaze for a few seconds, then seemed to snap back into work mode. She moved towards the door. 'Let's do it.'

Words he so wanted to hear her say. Just not about this.

They were in the large sitting room. He'd checked his blood sugar and taken a small shot of insulin. It was a fast-acting insulin that should start to take effect within ten minutes. But every patient was different. It could be up to thirty minutes. She would just need to wait it out with him.

'So, what do we do now?' He'd adopted his rock-star drawl. It was sexy as hell. But it wasn't the real Mitch. She knew that now.

She put her feet up on the table. Determined not to fall for any of his lines. She gestured towards the TV. It took up practically the whole wall. 'We could watch a movie or a TV show.' She shrugged. 'Listen to some music. Read a book.'

'You're being sarcastic now.'

She smiled. 'Am I? You just don't look like a book reader to me.'

He turned towards her more, hitching one leg up on the sofa and letting his arm fall behind her shoulders. 'And are you?'

She nodded. 'It's my secret addiction. Before my mum got sick I read a book a day.'

His body straightened up. 'Your mum is sick?'

She shouldn't have said that out loud. She was here to do a job. Not give away information about her family. She bit her lip. 'She had a stroke.'

'Is she better?' His words came out straight away and brought a lump to her throat.

She wasn't really sure how to answer. 'Well, yes and no. She's somewhere now that can take care of her.'

His brow wrinkled. 'Like a nursing home?'

Tears formed in her eyes. Why? She'd made her peace with this. She had. She'd spent weeks finding the best home for her mum and securing her a place there. But every now and then the overwhelming guilt that she hadn't managed to do the job herself chipped away at her.

'Is that why you're doing this job?' For reasons she couldn't explain, she just couldn't speak right now. So she nodded, and prayed that one of those tears wouldn't sneak down her face.

He reached over and grabbed her hand, encapsulating it in his own and squeezing it tightly. 'Being away at Christmas must be tough.'

She tried to paste a smile on her face as she blinked back those pesky tears. 'It's fine.' She shrugged her shoulders. Darn it. Now her voice had gone all wobbly. 'The holidays are always the best time of year to earn extra money. Lots of people don't want to work them.'

He was looking at her again. The top few buttons on his white shirt were undone and a few hairs curling up towards her. Her gaze was fixed there, even though she was willing herself to pull it away. He was still holding her hand. Still sending a little buzz up her veins. It was nice. It was more than nice. It was making her heart drum against her chest and beat out of sync.

He didn't let go.

'Why do you need to earn extra money, Sam?'

She flinched. It was too personal. No matter what he'd revealed to her today. She bit her lip. 'Doesn't everyone need a little extra money now and then?'

It seemed an innocuous answer but something flitted across his face. A look of distaste? She was trying to forget about her threat to quit today. She'd meant it. She would have walked away if he hadn't started to bend a little. But it would have caused her endless financial problems that she could really do without.

She pulled her mind back to the job. Back to monitoring Mitchell Brody for signs of his hypoglycaemic attack.

'How are you feeling?'

'Fine.' His answer was as quick as a flash, and he was wearing that sexy grin on his face again. 'Want to do something a little bit different?'

'What does that mean?' Her heart was giving the strangest flutter.

He walked over to a cupboard and pulled out the biggest stack of cardboard boxes—all brand new. 'You make a start on these, and I'll go and get the main event.' He walked over to the front door and pulled it open.

She glanced at the boxes and followed him to the door. What on earth was he doing? She watched as he opened the door to the nearby garages and started to wrestle the biggest tree she'd ever seen out through the garage doors. It was obviously much more awkward than he'd expected— the top part of the tree kept catching on the brickwork.

'Careful,' she shouted as she ran out to help, grabbing any part of the prickly branches she could get her hands on. It took careful manoeuvring. The heavy base had Mitch red in the face, with the veins nearly popping in his neck. Thankfully it was only a few steps back to the doorway. 'How long has this been in the garage?' she asked, as she tripped down the steps towards the lounge.

'Four days,' he muttered through gritted teeth. 'There!' With a huge grunt he wrestled the tree upright and into place next to the fireplace, before collapsing with laughter onto the rug below.

She sagged down on to the rug beside him. 'I thought you were getting some company to decorate for you.'

'So did I. But *somebody* told me I'd be missing out if I did that.'

She gave a little smile. Mitchell had actually listened to her. There was hope after all. She pushed herself upwards and slammed the front door to stop the icy blast coming into the house. She lifted the corner of one of the boxes and smiled, pulling out a ready-made red, green and gold garland for the fireplace. 'Do we actually have any real decorating to do?'

He gave her his lazy smile. 'I'm starting simple. Those ones we just hang up. But one of the boxes has the tree lights and the tree decorations. We have to do those ourselves.'

She couldn't help but grin. There was something so nice about that. She lifted down the next cardboard box and opened it. It was full of Christmas lights, gold stars and red berries. She lifted them out and started to try and untangle them. Mitch stared at her. 'What are you doing? Can't we just put them on?'

She shook her head and handed him the plug. 'No. You've got to be methodical about it. Haven't you ever decorated a tree before? We need to check the lights are working first.'

He hesitated for a second. 'We didn't really do trees in

our house. We spent most of the time at the hospital. There wasn't much point putting a tree up in the house.'

Her heart gave a little squeeze. It was time to ask the question that had been floating around her head. 'So, what's the story with the children's hospital? You said they looked after your brother?' She hesitated as she realised she'd never asked about the outcome for his brother. Mitch hadn't referred to him in the past tense, had he? Her insides started to cringe.

But Mitch just replied in a matter-of-fact tone. 'Shaun was sick for a few years. He had chemotherapy and radiotherapy but eventually needed a bone-marrow transplant. He was cured after that, and he's never had any relapses.'

He flicked the switch on the lights and they flickered on, a warm glow of gold twinkling stars and deep red berries. Sam gave a little gasp. 'Oh, these are great. Just leave them on while we put them up.' Should she ask the next question? This was the first time Mitch had really been open about his family. 'Who was the donor for the bone-marrow transplant, your mum or dad?'

He shook his head. 'Nope. It was me.'

She felt shocked. Of course she'd heard of sibling donations, but surely he'd been too young? She was starting to wind the lights around the branches. 'Come and help, I need an extra set of arms.' But instead of positioning himself at the other side of the tree, Mitch came around behind her, putting his arms around her back to catch the drooping coils of light. 'What age were you?' She tried to calculate in her head. 'You wouldn't even have been a teenager.'

He nodded, dropped the lights again and tugged at his jeans, pulling them down a little, revealing the upper part of his buttock and hip joint, 'I don't even have a scar,' he announced. Then gave her a wink. 'No war wounds to show the girls.'

He was trying to make light of it. But Samantha knew

better than that. She knew exactly how painful it would have been for a young boy to donate bone marrow to his brother—he'd probably spent the best part of a week in bed.

Her professional head was spinning. This had been twenty years ago. She knew exactly how things operated now—how they endeavoured to protect children—but had they been the same then? 'Did you understand what you were doing? Did you want to do it?'

He leaned towards her, picking up the coils of lights again and letting her inhale his woody aftershave. 'Of course I did. Shaun is my brother. I would do anything for him.' His eyes flickered with the recognition of what she meant. 'No one coerced me. No one made me do it.'

'And how is Shaun now?' They were moving slowly around the tree together, stringing the lights as they went. She was curious. He'd said his brother was well, but it wasn't Shaun that was here, visiting a children's hospital full of sick kids every afternoon. It was Mitchell. Why did he feel such strong ties?

He reached up to place the last string of lights near the top of the tree, his chest brushing against her shoulders. It should be too close for comfort. But it wasn't really feeling like that.

She stepped away, trying to keep her head in focus. She picked up the next box full of gorgeous red and gold baubles and blown-glass ornaments. 'These are beautiful, Mitchell. I've never seen decorations like this before.' They were mesmerising, and probably cost more than she earned in a month. Her mother would love these.

'It seems like you should have the honours of decorating your first official Christmas tree.' She started to pass them up to him one at a time.

'Don't you want to do it?' He looked confused. 'I thought that's what you wanted.'

'So did I,' she said quietly. 'But it's reminding me of how much I miss my mum.'

He paused, hanging the first few from the branches. She was lost for a second. Seeing the decorations like this was bringing a whole host of forgotten memories to mind. She could almost smell the cinnamon-scented candles her mum had used. He seemed to know to give her a little space, but she was conscious that the way he looked at her was changing. Her hands worked like clockwork, handing him one decoration after another, until the box was empty and the room was filled with lights glistening and reflecting on the glass ornaments.

The mood in the room had changed. He moved, coming closer like a prowling lion stalking its prey. He pulled her upwards from the rug and guided her over to the sofa, his hand plunking down on one side of her hip, the other reaching across her shoulders. Mitchell Brody was right next to her, the sides of their upper bodies and thighs touching. Way, way past invading her personal space.

'My brother Shaun lives in the States. He's married with two kids. Two unexpected bonuses.'

'What do you mean?' There were tiny little freckles just across the bridge of his nose.

'He'd been warned that his radiotherapy and chemotherapy could affect his fertility later in life.' He smiled. 'It seems he lucked out.'

Something clicked in her brain as he licked his lips and looked at her appreciatively once again. No one could predict what someone's hypo symptoms would be. Trembling, shaking hands were common. Some people became really quiet and withdrawn. Her sister had a slight aggressive streak. Mitch? It was beginning to look as if he had a flirtatious streak. Maybe low blood sugar meant that some of his normal defensive walls were slipping. This could be dangerous. She was trying not to read anything into this. She was trying to keep things normal.

'So, shouldn't it be Shaun who wants to pay it forward to the hospital, instead of you?'

He gave a lazy smile and shook his head slowly. 'You should get it, Sam. You're a nurse. St Jude's changed everything for our family. If we'd lost Shaun...things would never have been the same. We would have been damaged. We would have been lost. They patched us up when we were falling apart. You don't forget that. Not ever.'

The Christmas decorations sent a red and gold glow around the room, bathing them both in the warm light. His face was inches from hers. And a very handsome face it was too. His scraggy hair was falling towards her and she resisted the urge to reach up and touch it. Any minute now she'd talk him into checking his blood-sugar level.

Mitchell sighed and shook his head. 'You've no idea, Sam. None at all. One minute everything's fine in your world and the next...' he lifted his fingers and blew on them '...everything is just scattered in the wind.'

She swallowed. It brought back a whole host of memories. Blowing dandelion seeds in the wind had been something she'd loved to do as a child with her mother. She could almost see them floating around as they stood there.

He wasn't finished. It was as if the walls had come down on the normally guarded Mitchell Brody. 'I didn't know what to do. I heard words. I'll never forget one of the doctors telling my parents to prepare for the worst and that Shaun could be terminal. They think kids don't understand words like that. But when you're six—in a place like that—you learn very quickly what those words can mean. I was so, so scared. I remember the rage. It was like a red mist descending all around me. Uncontrollable rage.' He gave a little smile. 'And I wasn't that kind of kid at all. I ended up running out of the hospital and kicking a wall so hard I broke the bones in my foot. One of the nurses had to come and help me.'

'Oh, Mitch.' She reached over and touched his arm. 'That's awful.'

He couldn't look at her. She could see the sheen in his eyes. 'Back then Shaun was my world. We lived in each other's pockets. I mean, he's good now, he's healthy. We've both grown up and he's married with kids. I've got a totally different lifestyle from him. But the connection, and the memories from so long ago, they just never leave you. St Jude's gave us the lifeline we needed as a family. It feels like my duty to do that for other families.'

He held out his arms. 'I mean, look at me. The amount of money I get paid for playing guitar and singing? It's ridiculous. I'm the first person to admit that. But that's why it's so important that I keep doing something good with the money. Shaun doesn't earn anything like what I do. If the shoe were on the other foot, this is what he'd do with his money too.'

Sam was just listening, being as quiet as possible to let him speak. Her fingers were brushing the hairs on his arm. She whispered, 'I do get it, Mitch. I do. I might not have a sick brother or sister but I get that feeling of helplessness. I get that feeling of being out of control. I mean—I'm a nurse. I'm supposed to take care of people. I'm supposed to make people better.

'But I couldn't do that for my mum. I wanted to—I really did. But—' her voice cracked a little '—it's so hard. It's so different, taking care of your mum. I think I'm a good nurse, I do. But looking after someone else's loved ones is so different from looking after your own. I felt so guilty I could barely function. Any time she was sore, any time she was hungry or thirsty, I felt as if I wasn't doing a good enough job.'

He frowned. 'I don't believe that, Sam. You'd do a great

job with your mum. But it's impossible for anyone to be there twenty-four hours a day. How could you support her if you couldn't work?'

She pressed her hand against her heart. 'Maybe so, but it didn't feel like that in here. I always felt as if I could do better.' He pulled her closer and shifted a little. The weight of his body against hers made her slide a little down the sofa.

She was acutely aware of the heat of his body. It seemed to reach through the thin cotton of his shirt and wrap itself around her. She tried to adjust her position, but there was nowhere to go.

This didn't feel wrong—even though it should. He'd just shared something with her, and she with him.

He dipped his head, brushing his nose against hers. She caught her breath in her throat.

'So, Samantha. How did I manage this?'

Less than an inch. His lips were less than an inch from hers. She could feel his warm breath tickling her skin. It was delicious. It was playing with her mind. Making her lose focus.

'How did you manage what?' Her voice came out as a squeak. The lights on the tree started to flicker on their automatic timer. The natural light around them had been fading as they'd talked and the red and gold glow was practically the only light in the room. It made her think of old Christmas movies. And how did they all end?

The laughter lines reached up to his eyes, crinkling the skin around them in a warm, sexy manner. 'Manage to get the hottest nurse on the planet.'

It was definitely time to move. It was definitely time to take steps. Were his eyes a little glazed over, a little unfocused?

She would love to think that Mitchell had her pinned to the sofa because he thought she was the sexiest woman in the world. She would love to think that she was a star in her own personal Christmas movie where the little shop girl got swept off her feet by the millionaire businessman who'd never noticed her before, to the sound of some Christmas carol.

But every nurse sense told her this was no movie. This was an interesting case of hypo symptoms. Trust her to get the one patient in the world to get horny when he hypoed. This could get him in all sorts of trouble in later life.

She licked her lips and he growled. 'Oh, don't do that. It drives me crazy,' he taunted her, brushing his left cheek against her right. 'Have you any idea how good you look in these jeans?' This time he changed direction, dipping his head to the other side to brush alternate cheeks together. Her heart was racing in her chest. But part of her brain was still functioning. Was this all pre-programmed in him? Were these the moves he normally used around women? Because, truthfully, they were good. They were working.

His hair tickled the side of her face as his mouth approached her ear. She couldn't move. She just couldn't. Now his shoulders were pinning hers to the sofa. But she didn't feel scared, she didn't feel threatened. Mitch wasn't like that. He whispered in her ear, his voice a sultry growl, 'Have you any idea how much I've wanted to get my hands on you in those jeans?'

She cleared her throat. It was time to break out of the fantasy. It was time to be a nurse. No matter what the flickering Christmas lights were telling her.

But Mitch had other ideas. His lips trailed around her ear, dancing slowly across her face until they reached her own lips. Her natural instinct was to lick them again, moisten them as his mouth closed over hers.

It was only for a few seconds. But that was all it took. All it took to tip her world upside down and *kersplat* on the floor like an upturned trifle. Because, hypo or not, Mitch Brody was the *best* kisser she'd ever encountered in her life.

He didn't just kiss. He adored. He swept you away on a puffy pink cloud, kissing as if his life depended on it, and if he parted from you he would surely die.

She could almost hear the carol singers breaking into song around her and the movie credits starting to roll.

Enough.

She was losing her mind. All rationality, every sensible thought she'd ever had shot out the window as soon as his lips touched hers. His hair was tickling her face.

She pulled back, her head being about the only part of her body she could move.

'Mitch. Stop it. Get off me. Let me up.' She tried to bat his hair away but he laughed.

'Haven't you heard? Grunge is in.'

There it was again. The slightly glazed expression. His brow wrinkled and she arched her shoulders towards him to try and push him away a little. Only it didn't work. All it served to do was push her breasts up against the hard planes of his chest and bring the little twinkle that had vanished from his eyes for a few seconds rushing back like a freight train.

His mouth closed in on the pale, sensitive skin at the bottom of her neck. The one spot on her body that was guaranteed to turn her legs into a pool of mush. Just as well she was lying down.

At least this way she could move her hand a little. Dangerous waves of sensation were sweeping along her spine, nerves dancing with glee at a long-awaited touch.

How long had it been? Nearly two years? She'd been so busy with her mum these last few years that men had been the last thing on her mind. Maybe that was it. Maybe that's why her brain was on a murky spin cycle right now. Her body was finally revelling in the sensation of being touched again. And while selfish parts of her would like this to continue, professional parts of her were on complete alert.

She squeezed her hand between their chests and pushed him back. 'Stop, Mitch. Stop now.'

Her push had a little more force than she'd anticipated and he landed straight backwards onto the floor.

'Ouch!' The fall to the floor seemed to bring a little focus back into his eyes. The Christmas tree was directly behind him, the blinking lights sending his silhouette dancing across the wall. It was almost like being at one of his concerts.

She jumped from the sofa and knelt down next to him. 'Sorry. Are you okay?'

His gaze narrowed and he scowled at her. She stood up and held out her hand. 'It's time to check your blood-glucose level. How are you feeling?'

He ignored her hand and stood up with a little stagger. 'Fine,' he grunted.

She put her hands on both his shoulders. 'No. I want you to really think about it. Do you feel shaky? Sick? Hot? Any of the above?'

He shook his head. 'Just a bit, well...strange.'

'Good.' She led him over to the table and sat down in a chair next to him, pushing the meter towards him. She flicked the overhead light, sending bright white spilling across the room. He flinched. There. Much more appropriate. It would stop the Christmas movie tunes from circulating around her head.

He didn't speak. Just opened the meter, pulled a stick from the tub and loaded it. She breathed a sigh of relief. He still had enough of his faculties to know what he should be doing. His hands were trembling slightly as he used the finger-pricking device to draw a little blood. The tiny spot of blood seemed to be magically pulled from his finger into the stick as he touched it. It was amazing how little blood was actually needed. They both watched the ten-second countdown.

Four point zero. She stood up. 'It's official, Mitch. You're having a hypo.'

He glared. Again. 'Between four and seven is normal,' he grumbled. He was getting snappier, more argumentative. Good to know. It seemed he started at the amorous stage and moved from there.

'Between four and seven is normal for people who have been controlling their diabetes for a few months. I've told you this before. Your levels have been running higher these past few weeks, and it will take a little time for them to settle down. For you, right now, you hypo around four.'

His hands were definitely starting to shake a little more and sweat was forming on his brow. It was important that he recognise these signs. She sat down next to him and pulled over the supplies she already had ready. 'Look at your hands, Mitch. They're shaking.' She lifted his hand to his brow. 'And you're sweating. Do you feel it?'

'Of course I feel it. It's running down my back,' he snapped.

She ignored the snappiness. 'Good. These are things you need to take notice of for the future. Here…' She reached into the supply kit. 'There are some glucose tablets or a sugar drink in here. You need to take something to bring your level up quickly. What will it be?'

'I hate that stuff.' He pointed at the bright orange liquid in the bottle. 'I'll never drink it.'

'Try one of these, then.' She pushed the glucose tablets at him and he ripped open the packet and put one in his mouth.

It lasted around two seconds.

'Yuck.' He spat it into his hands. 'That's disgusting, powdery. I'm not eating that.'

He walked over to the kitchen and flung it in the trash can. She followed close behind. Under normal circumstances Mitch would never do something like that. But he was the same as most diabetics, all walls of reserve came tumbling down once the hypo started.

'What do you want, then?' She started looking through the cupboards. Her first idea had bombed. It wasn't practical to start making a smoothie like the last time—that had been a one-off situation. She needed to find something more accessible than that. Something Mitch could carry around with him that would act quickly.

'Chocolate.'

She blinked. He hadn't eaten any chocolate around her in the last few days. But if that's what he said he would eat, then that's what he would get.

She found some chocolate bars in a tin in one of the cupboards. She skidded one across the worktop towards him. 'This will have to do. Eat it now.'

He barely acknowledged her and it was worrying. His blood sugar would be dropping lower. Thankfully, Mitch wasn't the kind of diabetic to refuse to eat when it was obvious he was hypoing. They could be the absolute worst.

He ripped open the chocolate bar and ate it in two bites. All her instincts wanted to do everything for him. But this was about him learning, not her. She'd already learned everything she needed to about his symptoms. Now it was about teaching him what to do next. The chocolate bar was enough to bring his level up. It was time to be patient and give it a chance to work. Ten minutes should be enough. Then he'd need to make himself something a little more substantial. She'd already figured out that would probably be toast for Mitch. But he wouldn't always have her—or anyone—around when he hypoed. So he had to do these things for himself.

'I'm going to sleep,' he announced, walking over to the sofa he'd just had her pinned to and throwing himself down. Fatigue. Another late-onset symptom. Something else to remember.

She glanced at her watch and followed him over to the sofa. Not ideal, but she was here to watch over him. She'd wait ten minutes then give him a shake. If Mitch were on his own, this could be dangerous. Particularly if he didn't recognise the signs of hypo and didn't eat but instead just tried to sleep. She glanced at the timer of her watch again. Nine minutes to go.

But it didn't take that long. After seven minutes his eyes opened and he sat up and ran his fingers through his dishevelled hair. His forehead wrinkled and recognition crowded his eyes. 'Oh, no.'

She smiled. 'Oh, yes. Time to check your level again.'

He sighed and stood up. 'This is becoming a bit of a drag.' She followed him over to the dining table and watched while he checked his blood glucose, turning the monitor around to let her see. Seven.

'What now?' He rubbed his eyes. 'I feel as if I've done ten rounds in a boxing ring. I really could hit the sack.'

She nodded. 'It's not uncommon after a hypo to feel tired. What you have to do now is have something more substantial to eat. Something with more complex carbohydrates that will break down more slowly.'

He shook his head as if the weight of the world was on his shoulders. 'Toast.' He said it simply and moved towards the kitchen. His actions were mechanical. Putting bread in the toaster and finding butter in the refrigerator.

Then he halted, as if something had just lit a candle in his mind. His words came out slowly, deliberately, as if he was thinking about every one. 'I don't think dinner in Innsbruck is a good idea tonight. I'm not really feeling up to it.'

She stepped forward quickly. 'That's fine. No problem. Feel free to rest.' Her stomach had started doing flip-flops. He wasn't looking at her. He was deliberately looking away. Had he remembered what had happened between them? Remembered the kiss? Oh, no. Mitchell Brody wasn't embarrassed. He wasn't the kind of guy who would ever be embarrassed. But he might well be the kind of guy who felt guilty about his actions and regretted them.

Now, that would be humiliating.

She headed towards the door. She could check on him later. Do her nursing duties and forget about the whole thing. But Mitch wasn't finished. He put down the plate and knife in his hand and turned to face her.

'I get it. I get why you made me do this.' His sigh could fill the whole room. 'But I don't like it. I don't like not being completely in control. I don't like the fact that something like this could happen and I wouldn't be able to act to stop it.'

She moved closer, her fears forgotten. This was her job. This was why she was here. To educate, to reassure. It was time she learned to keep her mind on the job. 'But now you can. You got a little shaky, a little sweaty. You start to feel confused—unfocused. Now you know what you're looking for, it might make things a bit easier if it happens again.' She held up the meter and picked a chocolate bar out of the tin. 'You just need to make sure you have these on you at all times.'

'But what if I don't? What if I'm halfway up or down a slope and have none of those things?' His voice was different now, more vulnerable, and she could tell he was struggling with this.

She stayed firm. She pointed at the things again. 'It's simple. You don't ever leave home without them. You have to take charge of this, Mitchell. This is your body. This condition is manageable. You just need to keep on top of it.'

The words conjured up another kind of picture in her brain and from the rueful smile that danced across his face it was clear it had sparked a memory in him too.

His voice dropped. 'Shaky and sweaty weren't the only symptoms, were they Sam?'

She couldn't answer. It just didn't seem appropriate. She had wondered if he'd even remember. It wasn't exactly the most tactful thing for her to bring up.

'We can talk about this in the morning,' she said swiftly as she moved back to the doorway, her cheeks beginning to burn. She could still feel his breath on her cheek, the touch of his lips on hers, the brush of his chest against hers.

'Sam.' His voice sent a shiver down her spine. It was the way he'd said her name. As if it was honey on his tongue. As if he was caressing every part of her. 'I might hate everything about this, but I don't regret kissing you. Not for a single second.'

She didn't stop. She kept walking. Straight down the dark hall and into her bedroom, closing the door behind her before her legs turned to jelly.

What on earth had she got herself into?

CHAPTER SEVEN

TWO DAYS LATER Sam was still tiptoeing around Mitchell. They'd fallen into an easy routine. She didn't seem to have any problem getting up early and joining him on the slopes. Even though she categorically refused to set foot on the snow, she was happy to wait for him at the Seegrube mid-station.

It was even more of a relief that she had no qualms about going back to St Jude's every afternoon with him. Some of the kids even knew her by name already.

His phone beeped and he pulled it from his back pocket. *Can you call me?* It was Lisa. Their relationship was purely professional. She must be texting about one of the kids.

He pressed the dial button straight away. 'Lisa, what's up?'

'Thanks for calling, Mitchell. It's Brian. He became really sick last night. His dad had just flown out for emergency business in Dubai.'

'What happened?'

'You know he's been up and down. He spiked a fever really quickly. He's under emergency care and they've put him on the bone-marrow transplant list.'

Every hair prickled at the back of his neck. A deterioration like this could be deadly. He couldn't bear the thought that the young guy he'd played guitar with had become so sick so quickly.

'Is there a donor?'

There was a sigh at the end of the phone. 'Neither Brian's dad or mum is a good enough match. Nor is his brother. He's going to have to go on the general list.'

'Can I see him?'

'That's why I phoned you. Brian's dad has barely touched down in Dubai and is scrambling to get a flight back. His mum has flu and is holed up in the parents' room.'

Everything fell into place for Mitchell. 'And you've put Brian in isolation because his blood count is so low?'

'Yeah. He's isolated. We can't let his mum in. If Brian caught flu right now...' Her voice tailed off. She didn't need to say any more. Mitchell understood completely.

'I'll be there in fifteen minutes.' He hesitated. Should he take Samantha with him? But his brain was so fixated on getting there that he only gave it a few seconds' thought before he scribbled her a note and let the door slam behind him.

Half an hour later he was masked, gloved and gowned. Barrier nursing. More like space-age nursing. Luckily Brian was old enough not to be scared. Or so he thought. It was sometimes hard to remember that thirteen was still really a child.

Lisa was hovering around him. 'You're definitely not sick? There's nothing wrong with you?' Her eyes were scanning up and down his body. He could tell there were a million things going through her head right now—all of them about Brian's safety.

'Just say what you mean, Lisa.' He wanted to get in there. He didn't want to stand around a doorway.

'It's just...you've lost so much weight in the last few weeks. I know you say you're fine, but...well, it's not normal. Is there something you're not telling me?'

It didn't matter that he didn't want any of hospital staff to know what was wrong with him. It didn't matter that he didn't want any of them to think the tour was in jeopardy. He wasn't important right now. Brian was. And Lisa was asking all the questions an experienced nurse should.

'I've been diagnosed with diabetes in the last few weeks. That's why the rapid weight loss. Sam assures me it will go back on.'

The jigsaw pieces of recognition fell into place. He lifted his hand. 'Swear to me that you won't breathe a word.' He glanced through the glass. 'I've only told you so you won't worry about me being in with Brian.'

She gave a brief nod of her head. 'Now I know why Samantha's here. She told me she was a nurse.'

He put his hand on the door. 'Okay to go in now?'

She nodded, but she was still mumbling. 'Pity. I thought for once you might have found a decent girlfriend.'

He paused. 'What do you mean?'

She gave the slightest shake of her head. 'You know, one that doesn't care about fame and headlines.' She gestured with her head towards the room. 'Someone who knows what's important in this life. Someone with a heart.' She turned on her heel and walked down the corridor, leaving his brain whirling.

Was that what people really thought? That anyone who dated him only did it for the fame? It was more than an insult, it was a crushing blow. Mitch had always thought his looks and charm were the hit with the ladies. Most of the women he dated might not earn the same as he did, but they could certainly afford the life of luxury.

He thought back over the last few. Misty Kennedy had been fun for about ten minutes, but vain beyond all belief. She didn't eat. Full stop. And he didn't like it.

Carrie Beaulaux had been nice—if a little shallow. Truth was they just hadn't really had much to say to each other.

As for Lightning Adams, she was the true definition of a diva. Demanding and a control freak who seemed to have the press photographers at her beck and call. But the day that she'd spoken horribly to Dave, that had been her ticket out of there. He'd deposited her, her free designer wardrobe and her ten-thousand-dollar face cream on the sidewalk outside his LA home, just as a 'houses of the stars' coach tour was passing by. It might have made the headlines.

He watched Lisa round the corner at the end of the corridor. He liked her. He respected her opinion and the job she did. But it was the first time she'd ever made a straight mention of his rock-star persona. Much to his relief, she'd always totally ignored that. But her comment about Samantha bothered him.

Someone who knew what was important in this life. Someone with a heart.

It prickled every sense in his body. Was that why he was feeling the overwhelming pull towards her? At first he'd thought it was just his normal male hormones. Then he'd suspected a weird case of Stockholm syndrome. But maybe it was time to get to the bottom of this.

Maybe it was time to ask himself why a cute blonde with startling blue eyes was all he could think about these days. Was she the most gorgeous woman on the planet, with the best body? Maybe not in the world's eyes. But she was certainly looking good from his. He definitely wanted to know what lay underneath the array of cute jumpers and blue jeans.

But now wasn't the time. Now he had to concentrate on a thirteen-year-old boy who needed someone to hold his hand.

This young guy had reached a crisis point without his family support system around him. He'd be terrified. And Mitch understood. He just had to let Brian know that he did. There was no time to consider pretty nurses and blonde curls.

He pushed open the door and went inside. Brian's colour was so pale he was practically fading into the white sheets. He had an IV in place and his arm was littered with angry purple bruises.

He was so tired he barely lifted his head from the pillow. But the corners of his lips turned upwards. He recognised Mitch, even though he was hidden beneath a gown, cap, mask and gloves.

Mitch's heart gave a little surge. 'Hey, mate,' he said, sitting in the chair next to Brian and lifting his gloved hand to clasp the boy's.

This was why he did this. This was why he was determined to complete the tour. Nothing could get in the way of this.

Not even a beautiful nurse.

Sam's anger had only lasted about twenty seconds. Once she'd realised Mitchell hadn't just dived off to the slopes without her she dressed as quickly as she could. Her nurse brain was ticking. She grabbed extra supplies just in case in his rush to reach the hospital he'd forgotten his insulin and testing equipment.

The snow was much heavier today, the car tyres barely coping on the ten-minute drive. She wasn't used to this. Dave had assured her that driving wouldn't be a problem, but shouldn't she have those snow things on her tyres?

Lisa was panicking. Two of her staff were out with norovirus and the two replacements she'd tried to call were unavailable. She took one glance at Samantha and gestured her over. 'Mitch told me about the diabetes, so I know why you're here. But what do you know about cystic fibrosis?'

Sam blinked. 'Eh, quite a lot, actually. That was the job I was supposed to be doing before I took the job with

Mitch. I was supposed to be a specialist for a little boy with the disease.'

'So you've dealt with it before?' Lisa wasn't wasting any time.

She nodded. 'Yeah.'

'What about oxygen regimes and doing chest physio?'

She was beginning to sense where this was going. 'I'm fine with all that. Do you need some help, Lisa?'

Lisa turned the computer around and pulled up the web page for the UK national nursing body. 'Are you registered as Samantha Lewis?'

She smiled and bent over her, typing in her name and bringing up her registration status. 'That's me. Paediatric nurse and registered general nurse.'

Lisa turned to face her, desperation in her eyes. 'I wouldn't ask but...'

'What do you need?'

'Could you special a seven-year-old boy with cystic fibrosis for the next few hours until I can find someone else?'

Samantha nodded. 'I'm happy if you give me some background on the little boy.' She glanced down the corridor. 'I should check first. Is Mitchell okay?' Her fingers were jiggling the insulin pen in her pocket.

Lisa smiled. 'I put some food in the room earlier for them both. Everything should be fine.' She reached over and touched Sam's arm. 'You're good for him, you know.'

She was surprised. 'I am?'

'Take it from someone who's watched from the sidelines all these years. I was pretty shocked when he told me about his diabetes diagnosis. He might not give it away to the press, but Mitchell Brody is a control freak. I don't envy the job you have.' She gave her a wink. 'But I think you've got it covered.'

She waved her arm along the corridor. 'Now, come with me so I can find you some scrubs for the next few hours and give you a rundown on our patient. And, Samantha—' her grey eyes were serious '—I can't thank you enough for this.'

She felt a little flush of pleasure. She'd been looking forward to working this Christmas with the little boy she knew with CF. It was a real, hands-on nursing job. Sometimes she missed that. School nursing was great, very diverse with lots of social issues as well as health ones. But sometimes she missed doing the actual physical care.

It only took five minutes to change into a pair of pink scrubs and flat shoes. Lisa briefed her on the patient and she had a quick read over his notes. Rudy Jones had a lung infection, which was exacerbating his condition. The thick, sticky mucus in his lungs was making it difficult for him to breathe and his oxygen saturation was low.

'Hi, there, Rudy.' She walked into his room with gloves and mask in place. It was important not to introduce Rudy to any further germs. His defences were already low and his medication chart showed he was on two different types of antibiotics and some steroids. The bronchodilator that was currently running was causing little clouds around them.

She sat down next to the bed and spent the next ten minutes talking to him. He was frail, with an oxygen monitor attached to one finger. It was clear he was underweight— as a lot of the children with CF were because they couldn't digest certain nutrients in food.

It was easy to see how much strain his body was under. All the accessory muscles around his chest were working overtime. It was important to try and relieve some of the pressure on his lungs by loosening some of the mucus. Physiotherapy was a daily part of a CF child's life. Sometimes it could be fun, but sometimes it could be exhausting and difficult. Samantha was lucky. She'd had specialist training when she'd been a sister in ICU, so it meant she knew exactly how to help.

'Rudy, have you got a device to help with your physio?'

He nodded and pointed to the top of the locker. There was a 'flutter'—a handheld device shaped like an asthma inhaler—that delivered vibration to the airways of the lungs, making it easier to cough out mucus.

'Okay, we're going to start the active cycle of breathing techniques. Are you ready?'

He nodded and they moved the pillows on the bed to make him more comfortable.

She positioned her hands carefully to complement his breathing cycle of deep breaths, 'huffing' and coughing. She worked with him, vibrating certain sections of his chest with his huffing and coughing to try and loosen the mucus in his lungs and let him cough it up. It was a slow, painstaking process, with her monitoring Rudy throughout. He managed to expectorate quite a bit of mucus with the help of his 'flutter' device.

By the end he was exhausted—just as she'd expected he'd be. But his breathing was a little easier and his oxygen saturation had climbed a few digits. She wondered how Mitch was doing with Brian. Being with a kid like that would stir up a lot of memories for him. Here's hoping he wouldn't forget about his diabetes in the process.

His dedication here was much bigger than she'd expected. He showed real commitment to this place. And it was clear it was genuine.

When other stars were involved in places like these they usually had the paparazzi positioned on the doorstep or a camera crew filming their 'charitable' work.

Mitch was nothing like that. He was here because he wanted to be.

He was here because he cared. And it made her like him all the more.

She smiled at Rudy. Time to get the little guy to eat and increase his calorie intake. 'Okay, Rudy, what's it to be? Custard or chocolate pudding?'

* * *

Today had been the best day yet.

She'd managed to help a child when she'd needed to, and she finally felt as if she knew Mitchell a little better.

He wasn't the playboy rock star the media portrayed at all. He was sensitive, stubborn beyond all belief and had a serious, unwavering commitment to this hospital and its patients. She actually wondered if it was a little to his detriment. Was there something she didn't know? Obviously, there was.

Mitchell had been so focused on young Brian today he'd pushed everything else aside. She hadn't ignored her responsibility to him. And it was clear Lisa was wise beyond all measure. Any time she'd enquired about what was going on in the barrier nursing room, Lisa could tell her about food intake, blood sugars and insulin doses. It was clear, now she knew what was going on, that she understood completely. If Sam hadn't been happy that Mitchell was stable, she couldn't have helped with Rudy. Lisa had clearly been giving him 'prompts' as she'd dealt with Brian, in order to keep both her desperately needed assistants in place.

It wasn't as if she couldn't see into the room. She could. Young Brian had deteriorated quickly since yesterday, his colour and skin tone frightening. But she could see Mitchell—even if he didn't notice her. He was engrossed in talking quietly to Brian, entertaining him, being supportive.

One week ago she wouldn't have believed this. She would have searched around for the secret camera crew that must be filming Mitchell Brody doing his superstar 'good deeds'. But nothing could be further than the truth.

A regular nurse for Rudy had shown up around thirty minutes ago, just when she'd finished all the physio and then spent an hour trying to encourage him to eat. But she didn't mind. She loved working with kids. It made her feel useful. It made her feel worthwhile. This job with Mitch was the strangest she'd ever had. It didn't help that he was blurring a lot of lines for her.

He gave her a nod through the glass. It jolted her. She'd thought she might as well have been invisible. She held up the little sign she'd made, letting them know when Brian's dad's flight would land. There was no point in her going into the room and potentially exposing Brian to more bugs. The fewer people in his room the better.

Mitchell gave her a thumbs-up and wrote her a reply.

Dinner tonight in Innsbruck. 8 p.m.

She tried to ignore the flutter in her chest or the way her stomach just flipped over. He'd promised to take her out for dinner and show her around the city. Now that he knew when Brian's dad was arriving, it was clear he meant to see it through.

She tried to appear casual, giving the slightest nod and wave before strolling back down the corridor. What on earth would she wear? She didn't have any dressy clothes with her. She hadn't thought she would need any.

Lisa caught her puzzled look. 'What's wrong?'

'What do you wear to dinner in Innsbruck? It's minus four outside and I have no idea what to wear.'

'Something with an elastic waistband,' was the instant response.

Samantha smiled. Now, that did sound good. She hadn't had a chance to eat in the city yet. Most of the food in Mitch's house was very traditional. It would be nice to sample some of the local delicacies.

Lisa touched her hand. 'And definitely *always* leave room for pudding in Austria.' Her eyes ran up and down Samantha's frame. 'You know, I might have something I can lend you. We look around the same size.'

'You do? That would be great.'

Things were looking up. She didn't have any doubt that whatever Lisa had it would be perfect. Probably a hundred times better than anything she could have brought from home. She looked out of the window at the view of the city beneath them. The sun was beginning to set, sending a warm glow over the snow-topped roofs and coloured houses. The white-tipped mountain peaks seemed to blush pink at sunset. The lights in the houses underneath twinkled. It looked magical, as if anything could happen down there. The question was, did she want it to?

It was like having two mother hens pecking at him now. Mitch almost regretted telling Lisa about his diabetes as she'd clucked around him all day about eating, testing and injecting. And he really didn't like thinking of Samantha as a mother hen, because he had a whole host of other ways he could think about her...

It had been a whole week and he hadn't even taken her to the city yet. What an appalling host. His mother would be enraged. She'd brought her children up to have much better manners than that.

Tonight he would be the perfect host. Tonight he would show her the wonders of Innsbruck, all while trying to keep his hands to himself.

He left his black shirt untucked with the first two buttons undone. Mitchell Brody didn't dress up. He'd thought about taking her to one of the many local gourmet restaurants, before finally deciding to take her to one of his favourite Alpine inns. She'd never seen the Christmas market before and he wanted her to have time to wander around without being tied to a dinner reservation.

He glanced at his watch. It was only seven-thirty, but hopefully she would be ready early and they could head down the mountain. Now that Brian's dad had arrived, he felt as if he could finally relax.

It happened every time. Every time one of the kids he'd bonded with got sick, he couldn't get them out of his mind. The pale skin, the bruising, the lack of energy and appetite. Just like his brother.

It didn't matter that his brother lived a healthy life now. While they'd been there as children they'd seen other friends become sick and slip away. That reality was still there now, and he couldn't let that affect his work with the hospital. In fact, it made it much more important. Every family should feel supported, no matter what the outcome for their child. His tour money would allow that to continue in an environment more appropriate than they had now.

He'd been surprised to see that Lisa had persuaded Samantha to help out one of the sick kids. Lisa was wildly protective of her charges and the fact she'd relied on Sam, even for a few hours, was a big deal.

There was still that tiny doubt at the back of his mind— mainly stemming from the comment that Lisa had made. Samantha was clearly here to do a job. She'd already told him she needed the money. There was nothing hidden, nothing untoward. But was Samantha like the rest of the women Lisa had alluded to? If Samantha wasn't his nurse, would she only be interested in him because of his money?

He couldn't imagine for a minute that she was a fan or interested in the media. She hadn't made a single comment like that. But money could be a big draw for people. Maybe he'd made a fool of himself by kissing her the other night. She hadn't objected, though, and now it was eating away at him. Samantha seemed spunky enough to tell him not to make assumptions about her. He was cringing at the thought that he might have pushed himself on her unwillingly. Now he was beginning to doubt himself. Was the underlying attraction between them really there? Had it truly been there with any of his past relationships? Or had he just been too blind to see that women weren't actually interested in him, only his money?

It was the first time in his life he'd ever had thoughts like this. And he certainly didn't like the way they were playing on his mind.

Tonight would solve that. Tonight would let him forget about all that. Tonight would be about showing her around a city that he loved. It would be about introducing her to the local customs and traditions he'd known since he was a child. He ran his fingers through his hair one last time.

The smell hit her as soon as she stepped from the black four-by-four. 'Oh, wow, what's that?' She sniffed the air hungrily. The whole area around her smelt good enough to eat.

Mitchell grinned as he got out of the car. They'd been lucky to get parked as the streets were crowded around them. He moved out of the way of some locals and walked around next to her. 'That is the smell of Tyrolean fritters, mixed in with the smell of gingerbread and punch.' He held out his arm. 'Welcome to the Christmas market.'

She wrinkled her nose but couldn't stop smiling. 'Okay, you've got me. What's a Tyrolean fritter? And should I really be eating anything like that?'

'A Tyrolean fritter is the best thing in the world, especially if it comes with lingonberry jam.'

She shook her head as she pushed her gloves on her hands. 'I don't even know what a lingonberry is.'

He steered her through the crowds, past the floodlit white Imperial Palace set against the background of the Alps and the luminescent St Jacob's Cathedral swathed in a multitude of coloured lights. They almost took her breath away.

'Can we go inside the cathedral?'

He nodded. 'It won't be open right now, but we can come back during the day. Would you like to see around it?'

'Absolutely. I love buildings like this.'

As they walked through the streets the sounds of Christmas carols echoed around them. It seemed like the whole of Innsbruck was in the Christmas mood. The entrances to every door were covered in garlands of evergreen boughs and red velvet bows. Christmas-tree lights glittered in the windows all around them.

The Christmas market in the old town was magical. Stars and fairy-lights were strung across the streets. Figures from well-loved fairy-tales gazed down from the windows of the old town houses.

The smell of hot spiced wine surrounded them and they stopped at a large copper cauldron. Mitchell handed over some money and brought back two steaming cups. Just a sip was enough to catch in her throat and send a warm feeling down to the tips of her frozen toes.

'What's this called?'

He smiled. 'Glühwein. Any more than a cup will give you a major headache in the morning.' There were other stands all around them and the air was filled with a whole host of tantalising and unusual aromas. Even in the space of a few paces she could smell everything from doughnuts to roasted chestnuts, chocolate and candied apples and garlic bread. He stopped in front of the next stand with some shiny brown pretzels and stuffed fritters, carefully placing his virtually untouched glühwein to the side.

Four teenagers with bright pink candy floss wandered past them while they waited in the queue. Mitchell gestured towards one of the stuffed fritters, dusted it with sugar and wrapped it in a napkin before holding it out towards her. 'I don't want to spoil your appetite before dinner, but you've got to try this.'

He was holding the wrapped fritter with both hands and

she could smell the warm jam inside. She eyed the dusted sugar around it, 'Please, don't tell me this is one of your addictions?'

He laughed. 'Fortunately, no. But everyone who comes to Innsbruck at Christmas should definitely taste one of these. Think of it as one of the unwritten rules.'

She bent forward and took a bite. It only took the briefest seconds for the taste explosion in her mouth. The fritter wasn't heavy, as she'd feared. It was light and crispy, but the jam inside was much hotter than the mildly warm fritter. 'Ow-w-w!' she yelped, closing her mouth in shock, then opening it again quickly in the hope the cold night air would help with the jam burning her tongue. She panted, blowing out clouds of hot air into the icy night.

Mitchell was laughing, watching the steam rise from the fritter in his hand. 'Sorry, I should have warned you.'

It took a few seconds before she could speak, then she felt a drip of the still boiling jam slide down her chin. She took a deep breath and swallowed as quickly as she could, desperate to try and regain what was left of her dignity.

But Mitchell stepped forward, pulling his hand from his glove and catching the sliding drop with his finger. He did it so gently, so delicately that for a moment she felt as if she were in some expensive beauty parlour. He was so close, blocking out some of the coloured lights around them, leaving him bathed in a beautiful glow. His eyes were darker than ever and his frosty breath mingled with hers. He held up his finger, which was coated in rich red jam. 'Want to finish this?' he whispered, as he lifted the edge of the paper napkin and wiped it down her chin.

Her tongue darted out automatically, licking her lips and picking up the last delicious vestiges of jam. She shook her head.

She was finding it difficult to say anything. The closeness wasn't disturbing. It was tantalising. Just above his head was a string of white star lights. If this were a movie there would be electric sparks shooting off in the background.

'Good,' he said huskily as he put the finger in his mouth and sucked off the jam.

Oh, no. She couldn't start thinking thoughts like these. They were in the middle of a street, surrounded by hoards of other tourists and locals.

Street entertainers were playing cow bells and accordions, other locals were yodelling and doing traditional dancing, causing anyone nearby to start tapping their feet automatically. They walked towards another square, bustling and full of people with an enormous Christmas tree at one end, but it was the glistening above it that took her breath away. Golden glittering tiles on the roof of a three-storey-high balcony overlooking the plaza.

Samantha spun around. 'You mentioned this, didn't you? Wow, it's spectacular. It's not real gold, is it?'

The lights around the roof made the reflections from the roof glitter wildly. More coloured lights that were strung across the plaza bobbed in the wind. It made the reflections even more magical, blue, red, pink and green.

'They're gold-plated copper tiles. There's more than two thousand of them. It was built by some archduke in the fifteenth century.' He glanced towards her, his smile reaching from ear to ear, and his arm settled around her back. 'It's always more spectacular to see it first at night. Especially with all the Christmas decorations around.'

He was right. She could hardly draw her eyes away. All around them the flashes of cameras popped, sending even more reflections out into the night. She could stand here and watch this all night. Never mind the warm arm around her waist, resting on her hip bone and pulling her close enough to make her feel that she should actually be there.

It was like being in the middle of a Christmas card. All

around them were wonderful sights, sounds and smells. The Tyrolean folk seemed larger than life, friendly and welcoming with singers and musicians in all corners of the marketplace. Any minute now some fairy-tale king was going to appear on the balcony above. Out of the corner of her eye something flashed white. Was this one of the pro-verbial unicorns?

No. It was beautiful white horses, being led around the square with young children on their backs, part of another parade.

Mitch walked her backwards towards the façade of one the shops. She turned to peer through the window. It was full of candy canes and carved wooden objects, more tradi-tional items that just made her smile even more. Up in the chalet in the mountains she'd had no idea about the world of Tyrolean traditions down here. She would have to per-suade him to bring her back down here tomorrow so she could do some serious shopping.

'Come on.' He slipped his hand into hers. 'The inn will be busy. If we hang around too long we'll never get a table.' He pulled her through a labyrinth of alleyways until they reached the door of a white and black painted inn.

He pushed it open and she was immediately surrounded by warmth. She pulled the zipper on her blue ski jacket. The inn was crowded, but it didn't seem to be full of tourists, from the language around her, this inn was full of locals.

Lisa had chosen well. Her black sequined tunic over black leggings and boots was pretty, without being over the top. Sam was twinkling almost as much as the Christ-mas lights, and from the way Mitch was looking at her, he seemed to appreciate it.

They took a table next to the flickering fire. She glanced at the menu in front of her and shrugged. 'Well, I don't have a clue. I'm sorry to say I can't read a word of German.'

Mitch pulled off his jacket and hat, leaving his hair

mussed around his head. 'Would you like me to order for you?' He hadn't even looked at the menu.

She looked around. 'Do you eat in here regularly?'

He winked. 'That would be telling too many secrets.' He leaned back in his chair. 'I suggest some of the local cuisine. If I promise to bring you back another day to sample the cakes and desserts, will you trust me to order you dinner?'

She put her elbow on the table and rested her head on her hand, letting her eyes drift into the corner of the room. 'Will I trust you? Now, there's an interesting question...' She let her voice tail off.

The waiter appeared at their table, filling their glasses with water and nodding at the requests made by Mitchell.

She waited until he'd left then narrowed her gaze, 'Go on, then. Surprise me. What have you ordered?'

'All my favourites—fresh Bergkäse, Tyrolean gröstl and Plattin.'

She rolled her eyes as her stomach rumbled. 'Now, tell me what that is in a language my stomach understands.'

He laughed. 'Mountain cheese, roast meat and potato pancakes.' He pointed to her rumbling stomach. 'Believe me, you'll love it.'

There was a clink of glass as the waiter delivered a soda for Mitch and a glass of white wine for her. She raised her glass. 'Are you sticking to the diet soda?'

He nodded in response. 'I've only drunk diet soda...' he let out a sigh '...and I'm planning on giving alcohol a miss until I get this diabetes thing under control.'

She smiled, a little surprised. It was so nice to hear him say that. It was the first time he'd actually made a comment that made her think he was willing to do some work himself.

She took a sip of her wine. It was good, light and fresh, just what she liked. She sucked in a deep breath. Mitch had intrigued her today. There was more to him than met the eye—and she definitely wanted to dig a little deeper. Her head was trying to reason with her curiosity. If she knew him better, she could help him tailor his diabetes to suit his lifestyle. But that wasn't really why she wanted to know more about Mitch...

'So, Mitch. It's just you and me. I watched you today at the hospital. I can tell how much you care about these kids. But wouldn't you like to stay here a bit longer? Give yourself time to get more in control?'

She was trying to tug at his heartstrings. The thing she knew was important to him. Maybe it was a bit manipulative. But if it worked...

She kept going. 'Why are you so focused on this tour? Wouldn't it be simpler just to delay the whole thing until you were in better health?'

He shook his head. 'You make it sound so easy. It's anything but.'

She held up her hands. 'But why? You're Mitchell Brody. You've got the world at your feet. Don't you just click your fingers and everyone comes running?'

He let out a short burst of laughter. 'I wish!' He raised his eyebrows. 'You certainly don't.' He let the words hang there as he ran his fingers through his hair and rested his elbows on the table. 'This tour has taken two years to plan. Two years to iron out with my management and band members.'

She was trying not to smile at his first comment, but she was still confused. 'What did you have to iron out?'

He hesitated. 'Things are a bit different about this tour. It's not as straightforward as it seems.'

'Why?' She wasn't going to let it go. She wanted to understand if something about this was putting him under more pressure. It was an important factor in controlling his diabetes.

He couldn't seem to look her in the eye. 'My share of the tour proceeds and a certain percentage of the profits are tied up somewhere else. I mean, the guys aren't getting what they normally would on a tour.'

'Why?' She couldn't stop asking the question. The guy was a billionaire, did he have some kind of crazy debts? An uncomfortable prickle went down her spine. How well did she know Mitchell Brody really?

This time he did meet her gaze. Uncompromising. 'Because I asked them to.'

It was the way he said it. The sincerity behind his brown eyes. Every hair at the back of her neck stood on end as if a cool breeze had just blown past.

She could tell he wasn't going to say any more. His tone had more or less let her know the conversation was over. But it only succeeded in making her more curious than ever.

'What do you need the money for?' Her voice came out as a whisper, almost lost in the background noise and chat. There were deep furrows across his brow.

He didn't have time to answer before the plates were put down in front of them. It only took a few seconds for the wonderful aroma to engulf her. It wasn't the only thing to engulf her. A wash of relief was sweeping over her too. She'd asked a question she wasn't sure she wanted an answer to.

The frown on his forehead made it clear he wasn't happy with her comments. Mitch leaned forward and murmured what each dish contained. He picked up his knife and fork and started eating quietly. The silence was painful.

Things had been so much fun earlier, so festive, so flirty. She certainly knew how to create an atmosphere.

Panic started to flow through her veins. What if he decided to sack her? She needed the income for her mum.

This job was playing havoc with her senses. One minute she was threatening to quit and walk away, the next she was feeling panicked about getting sacked.

The truth was this should all be about the money—and

her responsibility to care for her patient. But, slowly and surely, this complicated man was starting to get under her skin.

The rational part of her brain started to kick in. She'd merely asked a few questions. Sure, she was curious about the personal stakes, but the initial questions had been based around his condition. That was fine. That wasn't a sackable offence.

She took a mouthful of food then sucked in a deep breath. It was time to take a different tack. 'What about practising, I mean, rehearsals for your tour? Shouldn't you be doing that now? Your tour starts in two weeks. Isn't this the time to be running about like crazy, doing all those sound-check things?'

The corners of his mouth turned up and his shoulders relaxed a little at her lack of showbiz knowledge. 'We've done all the rehearsing. We did it in advance as we all wanted to take some holiday time over Christmas and New Year. It was during the rehearsals that I became unwell.' He ran his fingers through his hair again. 'I just thought I was working too hard—becoming too focused on what we had to do.'

Pressure. Stress. Those were the words that jumped into her head. Always risk factors for diabetes. Was the tour putting him under undue stress? Because that could affect his diabetic control too.

She was a little surprised. 'But these are your songs. You know them back to front. I would have thought the rehearsals would have come easy to you.'

He smiled. 'Just because I can play the guitar and sing the song doesn't make it easy. There are hundreds of things that can affect a performance. Every arena is different and because of the amplification and the way it can affect the sound, we have to take all of that into consideration. We're constantly tweaking for every venue we'll play at.'

'But what about your health? Isn't that important to you, Mitch?'

The frown fell back into place. 'My health is the least of my concerns right now. I just need to be able to stay on my feet and complete this tour.'

The words made her feel uncomfortable. Her nursing instincts were firing shots across her brain. 'You're not making this easy. If I don't think you're fit I'll have to say that. I've got to be confident that you can keep your blood sugar under control.' She bit her lip, 'The truth is, Mitchell, I've seen you skiing and we've worked out how much carbohydrate you burn while doing that. We can tailor what you eat and how much insulin you take for that activity. But a two- or three-hour concert? I wouldn't even know where to start.'

She reached across the table and touched his hand. The pads of her fingers tingled as soon as she came into contact with his warm flesh. 'I'm worried, Mitch. The last thing I want is for you to have a hypo attack in front of thousands of fans. That would be a nightmare. Truth is, the timing of all this is really difficult. The first few weeks of diabetes should be about seeing how to work things around your normal routine. Once that is sorted, then we can look at how a performance affects your blood sugar and plan for that.' She gave her head a little shake. 'I hate to say it, but I really think the best thing you can do is cancel.'

'What?' His voice echoed around the room, and several heads turned in their direction. Sam felt herself sink into her chair.

He realised immediately what he'd done and lowered his voice, leaning across the table towards her, eyes blazing. 'I wasn't kidding when I said this had taken two years to plan, Samantha. You think I can just cancel and set this up for a few months down the line? Not a chance. These venues, these arenas are booked out nearly eighteen months in advance. The timetabling for the band is done even further ahead than that. We have commitments to record a new album. Frank, the drummer, needs surgery—even that's had to be fitted into our timetable. Cancelling this tour would be a disaster.' He paused. 'And not just for us.'

He was deadly serious and her brain was scrambling to decide how to handle this. No matter what she'd seen at the hospital today, Mitchell Brody was used to getting his own way. Like it or not, she was going to have to try and work in a way that fitted around his demands.

He was staring off into space again, lost in his own thoughts. She'd have to give this some consideration. She needed him to work with her, not against her.

His eyes locked on hers. She could almost see the shutters falling into place. If she couldn't turn this around it wasn't only dinner that was going to be a bust.

'We'll need to do some rehearsals. I'll need to see you perform for the whole length of the concert. And not just once. We need to do it a few days in a row to see if the overall build-up affects how much insulin you'll need. This is complicated, Mitch, I can't just make up these calculations in my head. We need to base it on real life.' She was bending. She knew she was bending. But she was still allowing for her professional judgement to say no.

His brown eyes fixed on hers. 'Fine.'

Just like that. No argument. No ranting. Each concession was taking a little less time. A little less effort.

Then it happened. He gave a little shudder, as if he was shaking off the black cloud around his shoulders. She saw him inhale deeply and his gaze softened and he tried to smile.

He leaned towards her. 'So, Samantha. What about you? How do you feel about being away for Christmas?'

Wow. What a turnaround. She felt a little uneasy. But it was probably best just to go with the flow.

She looked around the room with its evergreen garlands and red bows, the shimmering tree in the corner of the room. There didn't seem to be a single part of this city that didn't scream Christmas at you. The Austrians did Christmas like no others.

It did give her little pangs. It took her back to years gone by when she and her sister hadn't slept at night with excitement. Their mum had loved Christmas, their whole house full of brightly coloured tinsel. Nothing could beat that feeling of waking up on Christmas morning to see a stuffed-full Christmas stocking at the bottom of their beds. Even as an adult she missed that. No matter how silly it seemed.

She took a deep breath. The words were hard to say. 'My life has changed. This is how it's got to be. I know that my mum is somewhere she's being looked after. I have complete faith in them—and that's a big thing for me. Trusting someone else with my mum's care is hard. But I have to do this. Christmas is the most profitable time of year for agency nursing. The last few years I've been with a family, caring for a little boy with CF.'

'Like Rudy at the hospital?'

'Exactly. They were great. They made me feel like part of the family. His mum and dad really wanted to do everything for him, but they had two other kids to consider too. It made a huge difference for them to have an extra pair of hands they could count on. It meant the whole family could enjoy Christmas with no pressure. I enjoyed doing that for them.'

It was true.

'Yeah, but Christmas at a price.' His voice dripped with cynicism.

She shifted uncomfortably in her seat. 'Don't say that. I know what you mean. And, yes, his family could afford it. But the whole job, it just didn't feel like a job. It felt like being part of the family. And at this time of year that's important.'

He took another forkful of the stew and lifted his eyebrows. 'So what happened this year?'

'The little boy—Daniel—he was sick. He's in hospital.' A cool chill washed over her skin. She hadn't phoned Trish to see how he was and she should have. She'd been so wrapped up in Mitchell this last week that she just hadn't got around to it. What was wrong with her? She never forgot things like that.

Mitch nodded slowly. 'So Daniel's loss was my gain. That's why you were available to do this job.'

Her eyes met his. Was he being sceptical? Or just matter-of-fact? She wasn't entirely sure. It was almost as if he was trying to weigh things up in his mind, and for some strange reason she felt as though he was finding her wanting.

It was the oddest feeling. And this was nothing to do with her nursing skills. This was about her, and her methods. Her, as a person. Her goals. Her values.

She'd never felt like this before. Never been so much on the spot. But the bottom line was, yes, she was here for the money.

Would she really leave her mum at Christmas for any other reason?

Her Christmas agency shifts were the only reason she'd managed to keep her head above water these last few years. This way she paid her mortgage, paid her mother's mortgage and paid the nursing-home fees. They'd tried selling her mother's house to help with finances. But the market was dead right now and homes just weren't selling, and, the idea of selling her mum's house didn't sit well with her anyway.

This was the answer. This was the thing that she could manage to do.

So why did it suddenly feel so wrong?

The food in front of her had lost its appetising aroma. Her stomach was still empty but churning. She couldn't even force a sip of her wine.

With a simple few sentences he'd made her mind spin. This was all because she'd crossed a line. Without even meaning to, she'd mixed business with pleasure.

Sometimes it felt as if he was looking at her, *really* looking at her with something special in his eyes. More than just a friend. More than just a colleague. As for the kiss?

Who was she kidding? Half the females in the world probably wanted to be kissed by Mitchell Brody, and she was a fool if she thought she'd managed that through anything but default.

Sure, there was sometimes a twinkle in his eye when he talked to her. On occasion it did feel like he was flirting with her. But maybe that was just Mitch? Maybe she'd misread everything. Including the fact he'd murmured he didn't think it had been a mistake.

Her warped brain was letting her imagination run wild and she'd actually believed that Mitchell Brody could be interested in her.

It was time for a reality check.

Then something else struck her. If this tour was really so important to Mitchell, could there be a chance that he was playing her?

Trying to get her to say that he was fit to do something he might actually not be? Now, that worried her all the more.

That compromised her professional integrity. Something she really didn't want to happen.

This night had started out so perfectly, with so much promise.

But the course of one conversation just seemed to have killed it, and all the friendly tones, stone dead.

So much for the festive spirit.

CHAPTER EIGHT

WHAT WAS WRONG with him?

Samantha had spent the last few days tiptoeing around him. And no wonder. He was acting like a bear with a sore head.

Every day she met him halfway up the slopes, their coffee drunk in silence as she watched him check his blood-sugar level and administer insulin.

Afternoons were spent avoiding each other at the children's hospital. She still seemed happy to go there—in fact, it was the only part of the day she seemed to enjoy. She'd developed an even better rapport with Lisa, the rest of the staff and the kids, which made him seem even more unreasonable.

But he just couldn't get things out of his head.

And it was all his own fault anyway.

For the first time in his life money was keeping him awake at night.

Samantha was here because she wanted to get paid. She had no loyalty to him, or interest in him personally.

After she'd spoken about the other family she normally spent Christmas with—for a price, of course—he'd felt a lousy second choice. Something else that he wasn't used to.

First there had been the comments from Lisa about finally picking 'a good one', then there had been the implication that Sam was desperate for money. Almost as desperate as he was.

But it was worse that that. Much worse.

Because her lips, her skin, her curls were haunting his dreams. It was like having an impossibly ripe peach sitting in front of him that he couldn't touch. Even though he tried to forget about her, he couldn't.

Samantha Lewis had burrowed her way under his skin.

He was trying to stay focused. He was trying to think of a way to make sure he could keep on top of the diabetes long enough to get through this tour. Once he was at the end of the tour he could take as much time as possible to look after himself.

The worst thing was he wasn't in control. No matter what it looked like from the outside. He was trying his best, he really was. But last night he'd woken up shaking, with the bed drenched in sweat.

Thankfully, Sam had already warned him about nighttime hypos and there had been an easily accessible bar of chocolate next to the bed. He hadn't even waited to check his blood-sugar level. And, yes, he knew it was wrong. But he'd been gripped by an unholy terror. Usually, he was in his house alone. What if he hadn't woken up? What if he'd slept right through? Would he have been dead in the morning?

He couldn't face going through in the middle of the night and waking her up to tell her, because if he did, he might see her in that short satin nightdress again and start to imagine unthinkable things. He'd just slammed the chocolate down his throat and waited until he'd eventually stopped shaking. Then he'd stumbled through to the kitchen and made himself some toast. It was becoming his staple go-to food.

By the time he'd eventually got around to checking his blood sugar it had come up to six. He could only imagine what it had been before. And that scared him. That *really* scared him. The whole out-of-his-control element was unbearable.

But he just didn't feel he could talk to her about it. Would she understand? Would she care?

This whole thing had him tied up in knots.

But one thing did make sense. Whether she was only here for the money or not, she'd told him that they needed to assess how his time on stage affected his diabetes. At some point he was going to have to do a mock gig—probably more than one. Three hours of full-on stage performance, checking his blood sugar before, during and after.

The thought of it made him cringe. Why had this happened to him? The very last thing he wanted to do was collapse on stage in front of thousands of fans and be unable to perform. He could only imagine what the press would speculate about then.

That hypo last night was really playing on his mind. It had been his first experience of dealing with a hypo himself. Granted, Sam had only been down the corridor and had disaster struck she would have checked on him in the morning and intervened. But he couldn't rely on that. He didn't *want* to rely on that.

He wanted to be able to look after himself. He didn't want to be second-guessing himself every minute of the day—or minute of the night.

How on earth was he going to get through a tour if he didn't have things under control?

He sighed, leaning forward and running his fingers through his hair. He had to find a way through this.

He sat upright. Money. Maybe if he offered her enough money she would stay for the tour. It was four months, but she could travel with him, stay in luxury hotels and make sure his diabetes stayed on track.

But no. She had a permanent job back home. This was

her holiday time. And it was unlikely she'd want to give up her permanent job and travel the world for four months when her mum was in a nursing home back in England.

He let out a long stream of air from his lungs. What else was there? He could always find another nurse. But that thought appeared like a big black smoking cloud. Another nurse wouldn't have Sam's blue eyes, cute curls or even cuter bum.

She'd said that money was her motivating factor and he believed her. But he'd also heard how she'd spoken about her mum. Somehow he knew he could offer Samantha a big wad of cash and she still wouldn't want to be separated from her mum for too long.

Then there was the other stuff. The crossing-the-line, *I kissed her and wanted to do a whole lot more* kind of stuff. He groaned. What was wrong with him?

Mitchell Brody. See a girl, like her, ask her out. That's the way he'd always been. And for the most part it had served him well.

But this time was more than odd. For a start, he was sharing a house with said girl. He wasn't seeing her at gigs or occasional parties. For another, he wasn't entirely sure he was reading things correctly. They'd kissed. They'd flirted. They'd said things to annoy each other. So why was this different from any other time?

The diabetes was like a floating elephant in the room. He wasn't sure he could handle this on his own. In fact, he was quite sure that in these early stages he couldn't.

But he didn't want Sam here because of his diabetes. He wanted her here for *him*.

Ugh. His brain wasn't helping. Nothing made sense to him any more.

He walked over to the window and looked out at his precious mountains. It was only a few days until Christmas. Maybe he'd been harsh the other night? She must be missing her family. And maybe he'd taken her comment too personally about how special Christmas was with the other family. Of course Christmas was special for kids. That's exactly the way it should be.

Something pricked in his brain, sending a smile across his face. That's it. That's what he'd do. He already had plans at the hospital for Christmas. But maybe if he could make her see that Christmas was special here too, she might just start to come round. She might *want* to be around him, rather than feel obliged to be.

He couldn't rationalise why that was important to him. He just knew it was.

She hadn't seen the outdoor ice skating rink yet in Innsbruck. That's where he'd take her tonight. She'd already been impressed by the Christmas market, golden roof and cathedral. It was time to show her what the rest of Innsbruck had to offer. That's what he'd do.

Enough of the awkward silences. It didn't matter that they'd mainly been his fault. He needed Sam onside badly. And if charm was the way to do it, then Mitchell Brody could certainly oblige. Charm was easy. Charm was slick. He could do that.

He would play nice. He would do everything she wanted. Then, when the time was right, he'd suggest to her that she might want to work with him a little longer.

Of course he would pay her. He would never let her be out of pocket. But it was more important that she *wanted* to do it rather than *had* to do it. The money should be a nice bonus, not the deciding factor.

He could even offer to fly her home every other week to see her mum.

He made a quick call. Done. A large hangar booked for between Christmas and New Year to practise his set for the tour. That would give them a guide to how much energy he used during a performance. Hopefully it would be enough to tailor his food intake and insulin. It was so important that Sam said he was fit to continue the tour. Anything else would be a disaster.

In the meantime, he would do everything possible to keep her sweet. It wasn't as if that would be a struggle. Samantha was a honey. If he could just get her to leave her nurse's hat at the door, she could be a whole lot more.

There. Much better. He started to pull some clothes from the cupboard. It was time for him to pick himself up and start putting his plans into effect.

His gaze swept across the distant roof of St Jude's. He was doing this for the right reasons. Of course he was.

So why did he still have an uncomfortable feeling churning in his stomach?

She was living the dream. And ultimately it was her nightmare.

She was the invisible presence in his home. It was like being a ghost. Or, even worse, an unnoticed servant, which, in fact, she was.

He probably wouldn't even acknowledge her if she ran screaming through the house naked. The thought had crossed her mind.

What on earth was wrong with him?

She may have asked him a few difficult questions, and made a few suggestions he didn't like. But that didn't mean he could completely ignore her.

She was here to do a job—and she couldn't do it if he wouldn't communicate with her.

But it was more than that. Even if she didn't want to acknowledge it.

It annoyed her—embarrassed her even—that she still felt a little starstruck around him. She shouldn't, of course she shouldn't.

She was dealing with Mitchell Brody, patient, not Mitch-

ell Brody, rock star. She'd already learned that most of the
assumptions and gossip about him in the press was just a
smokescreen.

But what really annoyed her was the kiss.

The way it had made her skin tingle. The way it had conjured up a whole host of fantasies in her mind about how it
could have continued. And how it had ruined practically
every night's sleep since.

There were moments she spent with Mitch when she
felt they really connected. When she felt he might actually be interested in her, Samantha Lewis. She wasn't just
the convenient female presence in the house. She wasn't
just the hired help.

And it was those little moments, those knowing smiles
and locked gazes that made her stomach flip flop.

She kept telling herself this was crazy. Her mixed-up
head was reading things that weren't really there at all. It
had been one kiss. Just one completely perfect kiss.

But right now it felt like in fifty years she would still remember it. Still remember the feel of his skin against hers,
the brush of his hair tickling her cheeks, the intensity of
the look in his eyes. How many other women had lived out
their fantasies in the Mitchell Brody experience?

She shook her head. No. She didn't even want to think
about that.

That was horrid. That was painful. That was…

'Sam?'

He was standing in the doorway, dressed in a black
leather jacket, jeans and boots. She scrambled to sit up on
the bed, pushing away the pillow she'd been lying against
and pulling up the wide-necked T-shirt that had fallen down
one shoulder.

'Do you want to go to the hospital?'

It seemed the safest assumption. He certainly didn't
seem to want to spend any time around her.

He shook his head and walked into the room. The indignant part in her chest wanted him to ask her permission to enter her room. The self-conscious part was running her tongue across her teeth and trying to remember if she'd actually put any make-up on today.

How did he make a pair of jeans look so sexy?

He sat down on the edge of her bed and looked at her red-painted toenails. 'I think our differences in opinion might have affected my manners the other night.'

You don't say. Was he about to make an apology? Because he just didn't seem the type.

This was probably the time to bite her tongue and stay quiet. But that had never been in Sam's nature. 'I'm your nurse, Mitch. You don't have to like what I say, but that won't stop me saying it.'

'Yeah, you're my nurse.' He stared out of the window towards the perfect white snow. If he mentioned he wanted to go skiing she might pick up her nearest shoe and throw it at him. Climbing up a freezing mountain was *so* not what she wanted to do right now.

His hand reached over and touched her foot. Her first instinct was to flinch and pull it away, but he was holding on, not tightly, just enough to keep it in place. 'It's Christmas in a few days, Sam. I feel as if I haven't been very hospitable. You asked me to take you down to Innsbruck shopping—I haven't even done that.' He shook his head and let out a laugh. 'Have you any idea how much trouble I'd be in with my mother and Granny Kirk if they knew?'

She smiled. She couldn't help it. 'You make it sound as if you do what your mum and gran tell you.'

He rested his elbow on the bed, his chin near her knee. 'Disobeying Granny Kirk could result in a fate worse than death. No one, but no one ever argued with that woman. As for my mother, she has the best disapproving stare in the world. Award-winning. She's also the master of the tut.'

'The tut?'

He nodded, his face deadly solemn. 'Oh, yeah.' He made the noise with his tongue and shook his head along with it. 'That tut is actually about five hundred disapproving words all rolled into one.'

He smiled at her. Really smiled. She was being white-washed with his teeth. His whole face could light up with that smile. How many other women in the world would love to be on a bed with a smiling Mitchell Brody at their feet?

The thing was she didn't really care about any other women. She just cared about herself.

Oh, for a pair of stiletto heels, a perfect fake tan, a de-signer figure-hugging dress and sultry red lips. Wasn't that the kind of woman he was used to? Darn it. She'd forgotten the thirty-two double-Ds.

Nope. She was Samantha Lewis. Unruly blonde hair. A bit of tinted moisturiser if she was lucky and some cherry lip balm. Her current jeans were from the supermarket, along with her push-up bra.

But Mitchell didn't look as if he cared. He was crawling up the bed towards her.

'What do you say you let me be the host with the most?'

'Most what?' Her voice came out in an embarrassing squeak. Her brain was in places it shouldn't be. But then again, she was on a bed with Mitchell Brody, so maybe her current fantasies weren't as far-fetched as she suspected.

He reached the top of the bed. Planting one hand on ei-ther side of her, positioning himself directly above her. She was having flashbacks to that night on the sofa. It was all she could do not to let out an involuntary moan.

The beaming grin was still in place, and that twinkle in his eye she'd spied on a few occasions was definitely back. The guy was playing with her.

And, what was worse, she kind of liked it.

Their faces were inches apart. His hair fell forward,

tickling her cheekbones, his warm breath making her skin tingle. He knew. He knew exactly what he was doing.

Those deep brown eyes were drawing her in, taking down her defences like a swirling whirlpool with no chance of escape. And she didn't want to.

He bent closer. She held her breath. For a second she was sure he was going to kiss her. Just like he had the last time. Her body was craving his touch. All she wanted was to feel his lips on hers.

But instead he whispered in her ear, 'The guy with the most beautiful girl in the world.'

It would be so easy. So easy to believe that and drink in every word.

But the truth was the words fell a little flat. Because she knew—the whole world knew—the kind of girl Mitchell Brody usually had on his arm.

But the thing was, he was looking at her as if she *were* the most beautiful girl in the world. She could almost believe it.

His lips brushed against the tip of her ear as his face appeared back in front of hers. 'How about some fun?'

She could feel herself pull back against the comfortable mattress, her eyes widening. This was beginning to feel like some crazy daydream. Maybe while she'd been lying on the bed she'd actually fallen asleep. In a few moments she would wake up and realise it had all been a dream.

But the warm breath on her skin wasn't a dream. Neither was the persistent smile in front of her eyes.

'Let's go back into Innsbruck. I haven't shown you around much. I know you hate skiing, but what about ice skating? There's a rink right in the middle of one of the markets, we could go there. And shopping? Would you like to get some things for Christmas? I haven't got you a present so how about you choose something?'

Definitely a dream. He was making it sound like she

was about to get free rein on a credit card. She moved her foot, pressing her toes hard against his outer leg. Nope. He was still there.

She could smell him. She could smell the leather of his jacket. His aftershave was drifting around them, mixing with the smell of his shampoo. 'What do you think?'

This time his stubble scraped the edge of her nose. This was no dream.

She blinked, trying to decide what to say, trying to decide how to act. He was practically on top of her but she still felt as if she was misreading signals all over the place. If he'd wanted to kiss her, he could have. But he hadn't. It was almost as if he was wanting her to take the lead.

Should she?

She pressed her lips together, feeling the lip balm between them. Her tongue slipped out, an automatic reaction to what was going on in her brain.

His eyes caught the flicker of her tongue and she felt his body stiffen above hers. Then more, a natural male reaction started to take place. She couldn't help it, her smile was reaching from ear to ear. 'Is this how you ask all the girls to come and play with you, Mitch?' she quipped.

He threw back his head and laughed, flipping over and landing on his back next to her on the bed. There was no point trying to hide what had just happened. The evidence was there.

He turned his face towards her, both of them lying on the comfortable pillows. 'You're making this difficult, Sam.' He shifted again, leaning his head on his hand. 'What do you say?' The twinkle was getting sparkier by the second. 'Do you want to play with me or not?'

How to answer. The air was rich with innuendo. She could either fully embrace it or kill it stone dead. And nothing about this was straightforward. Her senses were on overload. Her hormones could currently light up the Christmas-tree lights for the whole of Innsbruck.

She wanted to tease him. She wanted to play him at his own game. She didn't care about the models or his past gorgeous girlfriends. What she cared about was that right now Mitchell Brody was interested in her.

She turned on her side to face him, lifting her finger to the little gap in his shirt where she could see a few curling hairs. She laid her finger on his skin. 'Well, that would de-pend.' She was smiling. She could see his reactions to her one solitary touch.

'Depend on what?' he growled.

She kept her voice low, almost a whisper. 'Depend on how things progressed.' Had she really just said that out loud? It almost sounded as if she was propositioning him.

This time it was he who licked his lips. She liked the effect she was having on him—the direct effect on his erogenous zones. It made her feel in control. It made her feel important.

'Well, what do you want to happen, Sam?' He was hold-ing his breath. He was waiting to see what she might say.

The million-dollar question, and all the power was in her hands.

How brave was she? She moved her lips closer to his and whispered.

'Let's find out.'

CHAPTER NINE

THANK GOODNESS FOR interruptions. Dave rang the bell a few moments later and they both jumped apart. She could barely breathe and her heart was thudding in her chest.

Mitchell pulled himself together first as she straightened her clothes. When he padded back to the room a few minutes later it was with a rueful expression on his face. 'That was Dave. Dropping off some groceries.'

She'd already collected herself and pulled on a jumper and some boots. She gave him a bright smile. 'Ice skating, then?'

He rolled his eyes and nodded, picking up his discarded leather jacket from the floor. 'Ice skating it is.'

Being around Samantha was a pleasure. The diabetes stuff wasn't even annoying him as much any more. She didn't need to prompt him. When they sat down for coffee he pulled out his meter and checked his level, she glanced at the screen and said nothing, letting him adjust his insulin dose himself, taking into account what he was about to eat.

If he'd been doing something wrong she would tell him. Sam was no shrinking violet. But this way he felt more in control. She didn't feel so much like his nurse, more like the girlfriend he was beginning to imagine her being. If Dave hadn't interrupted them…

The ice rink was busy, full of stumbling families and the occasional pro weaving their way through the falling bodies. He finished fastening the skates he'd just hired. Years ago he'd fancied himself as a speed skater for about ten minutes. He could skate. But the type of blades on these hire skates were different from what he was used to.

He watched as Sam finished fastening hers and stood up. She didn't hesitate, just stepped out onto the ice and skated straight to the middle, stopping herself by spinning around. 'Come on, slowcoach!' she yelled.

Mitch didn't need to be told twice. He crossed the ice in a few seconds and circled his hands around her waist. His stop wasn't quite as elegant as hers, but he managed to stay upright.

'Is there something you haven't been telling me, Samantha Lewis?' he murmured as their noses touched.

She pushed backwards, skating a little away from him before pushing off and twirling round a few times with her hands in the air. 'I can't imagine what you mean,' she said wickedly.

He slid forward, grabbing her around the waist again and pulling her tightly against him. 'So what were you? The ice-skating princess? The champion twirler?'

'All of the above. I might have done figure skating for a few years.'

'How many years exactly?'

She started skating backwards, lifting up her foot behind her, above her head and catching the bottom of her blade with her hand and spinning around.

'What on earth is that called?'

'A Biellmann spin.' She winked. 'It requires great flexibility.' She was teasing him again. And it made his heart thud a little quicker in his chest.

Sure, he'd been physically attracted to his partners in the past but Sam was different. It wasn't *just* physical attraction, and that's pretty much what it had been for the rest of his conquests. That, and publicity material.

Everything about that went against his principles, but when he'd started in this business and the band had been trying to make a name for themselves he'd more or less done whatever the management team had advised. If that had meant dating one pretty actress or model after another he'd decided it wasn't too big a strain.

But over the last few years he'd grown frustrated. He didn't want to be on display. There were parts of his life he wanted to keep quiet—including his work with the children's hospital. He didn't want to play games any more.

Sam was different. The only agenda she had was money. But it wasn't as ruthless as that. She had good motivation for what she was doing. It was obvious she struggled with the fact her mother was in a home. If this was the way she had to supplement her income to ensure her mum stayed in the best place possible, he really couldn't fault her for that.

But could he trust her?

Would Sam sacrifice other things for money?

Years ago, one of Mitch's old school friends had sold a story to the press about his brother's illness. Up until that point no one had known. It had blazed across the headlines for a few days then, thankfully, disappeared. There wasn't much interest in a brother who'd survived and made a good recovery.

But Mitchell hadn't forgotten the betrayal. It had been a hard lesson. Desperation for money could put people in a situation where consequences seemed unimportant.

He couldn't afford that to happen. He couldn't afford St Jude's and its patients to be subjected to unending press interest and speculation. The sanctuary of the specialist hospital would be ruined for the kids and their families who relied on it.

But could he trust Sam with his secret? Everything about

her said yes. Her attitude, her unwavering sense of right and wrong.

His initial plan to win her round by charm and casual flirtation was sitting really uncomfortably with him now. There wasn't any question that he'd do anything to keep this tour on track, but using Sam just seemed so wrong.

He liked her. He more than liked her—that was the problem. But he couldn't allow his growing feelings for her to cloud his judgement. If he let his heart rule his head it could be disastrous. What if she didn't feel as strongly about him? What if she was starstruck by the whole idea of being around someone in the media? He hoped not. He really hoped not. But the trouble was, he just didn't know.

He couldn't take the chance and he hated it that he had these little doubts about Sam. But he'd only known her just over a week. It wasn't enough time to really get to know someone well. All his instincts told him she was a good person.

He'd already had comments from Lisa. Dave seemed to like her too. People he respected and trusted.

He tried to shake it off. This was his problem, not hers. This all came down to the fact that she'd been honest and told him she was only here for the money. He couldn't judge Sam because of the betrayal of another friend years ago.

She might have only been here for the money originally, but what about now?

She was still pressing up close to his chest, the two pairs of skates making small movements on the ice. She smiled up at him, her blue eyes and blonde curls peeking out from under the bright blue hat.

Her cheeks were flushed from the exertion of her skating, or maybe from something else. He could stay here all day with his arms tightly around her waist, but the ice rink was busy with kids and families. He interlocked their fingers. 'Go on, then, take me a few times around the rink.'

He was laughing at her, knowing he could match her pace for pace. But it was nice to let her take the lead as she pulled him forward, weaving expertly between the skating and stumbling bodies until eventually they ended up at the exit again.

'So what did you think?' he asked as she unlaced her boots. She ran her finger along the blade. 'Well, they're definitely not what I'm used to—these skates are blunter than a wooden spoon.'

He shook his head as he picked them up to return them to the hire booth. 'Okay, you missed out on dessert last time we were here. Fancy some good Austrian coffee and cake?'

She nodded enthusiastically and he grabbed her hand, weaving through the winding streets towards his favourite café. She stopped at a few windows, gazing in at some of the items on display. 'Want to go inside?'

She shook her head and they drifted forward. Her footsteps slowed outside one of the designer women's clothes shops. He was conscious of the fact he'd offered to buy her something but she didn't seem to want to take him up on the offer. Her eyes had fixed on a gorgeous red dress in the window. He rested his chin on her shoulder. 'I think you would look spectacular in that.'

She started out of the daze she'd been in and shrugged her shoulders. 'It's not like I would have anywhere to wear something like that. It's much too elegant—too impractical.' She stomped her boots on the ground, knocking snow from them. 'I'll stick with the boots and jacket you already supplied. That's more than enough.'

Her eyes drifted towards the shop next door, where display cases of exquisite jewellery were on show, all made by the master craftsman inside. It was difficult to know what had caught her attention. The window was jammed full of gold and silver jewellery, along with glittering coloured gemstones. He smiled. His last lady friend would have fixated on the massive pink solitaire diamond at the front of the display. But Samantha's gaze was nowhere near there.

She shot him a smile and tugged at his hand. 'Okay, enough window-gazing. Let's find this coffee shop. I'm starved.'

He couldn't stop his eyes lingering on the window as he walked past. What was it that had caught her attention?

He pushed open the door of his favourite coffee house. The smell of rich coffee, steamed milk and succulent cakes surrounded them instantly. Samantha pulled off her gloves and rubbed her hands together, her eyes sparkling. 'I love it already.'

She went to sit down at one of the tables but he caught her elbow and guided her over to the huge glass cabinet with all the cakes on display. 'Have a look first and see what you like.'

Her eyes widened at the huge array of cakes and desserts. She shook her head at the small signs in front of each of the delicious-looking cakes. 'You're going to have to tell me what they all are. I don't have a clue where to start. We could be here all day.'

He nodded and pointed towards the cabinet. 'We'll start with the most traditional.' He gestured towards a rich chocolate cake. 'That's Sachertorte, a chocolate cake with apricot jam filling, probably the most famous—you'd usually eat it with whipped cream. Among the cakes with the longest tradition is the Linzer Torte. The one next to it is caramel-flavoured Dobostorte, the cream-coloured cake is Esterhazy Torte—it's really a Hungarian cake, buttercream spiced with vanilla sandwiched between layers of almond meringue.' She smiled as he continued down the cabinet.

'There are also the traditional pastries with fresh fruit and cream, and then there's Punschkrapfen. You might like that—it's a classic Austrian pastry, a cake filled with cake crumbs, nougat chocolate, apricot jam and then soaked with rum.'

She folded her arms across her chest. 'You seem to know a lot about cakes. Should I be concerned?'

He laughed. 'I've pretty much sampled everything in that cabinet at least a dozen times. But you've got to remember I've been coming here since I was six. I'm a cake connoisseur.' He gave her a wink. 'But my true downfall is the coffee in here. It doesn't matter what you pick, there isn't a bad one.'

She hummed and hawed around the cabinet before finally throwing caution to the wind and choosing the traditional chocolate Sachertorte with whipped cream. Mitchell was much better behaved, choosing a light pastry with fresh fruit and some low-fat cream. He ordered coffee for them both and it was only a few moments before the frothed milk concoctions appeared before them.

The sun was just beginning to dip outside and the Christmas lights were coming on all around them. He watched as she tasted the delicious chocolate cake and let out a little sigh. 'Oh, I can tell why you keep this a secret. It's gorgeous.'

He sipped his coffee. She was licking cream from her lips and it was playing havoc with his senses.

He glanced at his watch. He still wanted to visit the hospital again, but he'd had an email from his manager letting him know the insurance company was looking for a report on his diabetes. There was only one person they could ask for that report. Sam.

'Have you checked your emails today?' His insides turned over as he said the words. She was still concentrating on the cake, licking some chocolate from her spoon.

She shook her head. 'Nope. Should I have?'

He was about to do something wrong. Every cell in his body told him not to try and manipulate her, but his protective instincts towards the hospital just couldn't be smothered. Now he knew what being caught between a rock and a hard place was actually like.

He slid his hand across the table and intertwined his fingers with hers. 'I think you'll get asked about me soon.'

'Asked what?' Furrows appeared along her brow.

He tried to appear casual, but the handholding kind of negated that. 'About how I'm doing—if I'm fit enough to do the tour.'

'Oh.' The fork she had poised in her other hand was gently laid on the table. Her eyes focused on her coffee and she lifted it up for another sip. It was obvious she was trying to think of what to say.

All her reservations were practically on display. She hadn't pulled her hand away, but he knew she was currently questioning his motivation. Was he interested in her or the tour?

Both. He wanted to say the words out loud. But didn't want to see a glimmer of hurt in her eyes.

She tried to paste a smile on her face. It pained him. With Sam, he was used to the smile lighting up her eyes, but this time it wasn't there.

'Well, I guess it's time for me to see you rehearse.'

'What do you mean?'

She shrugged. 'We've already spoken about this. Keeping your diabetes under control in everyday life is different from performing on stage. I need to see you rehearse. I need to see how much energy you use up and the effect on your blood-sugar levels. That way, we can tailor what you eat and how much insulin you take before you do a show.'

Everything she said made sense. He knew that it did. But it didn't stop his stomach from churning. That little element of not being in control. He wanted to wave all this off and just say he would be fine.

He'd be even happier if Samantha thought that too. But it was quite clear she didn't.

She bit her bottom lip. He could tell she wouldn't be moved on this. She wouldn't compromise her professional integrity no matter how much he flirted with her or tried to keep her onside.

He tightened his grip on her fingers, giving them a little squeeze. 'And if we practise and everything's fine, you'll tell the insurance company?'

She pulled her fingers out of his grasp. Her voice was steady. 'If everything is fine, I'll say so. But if I have concerns, I'll also let them know. I'm not going to lie for you, Mitch.' There was the tiniest waver in her voice. As if she was struggling with being put in this position.

That was his fault. If Samantha was just his nurse, she wouldn't struggle with this at all. She'd be professional through and through. But he'd crossed the line, he'd kissed her, and that had messed with both of their emotions. Including the ones that were currently building in his chest.

'I don't expect you to lie for me.' The words came out angrier than he'd meant them to. But the truth was he *did* want her to lie for him. He wanted her to assure the insurance company that there was nothing to worry about and the tour was safe.

There was no question about his ability to perform. The only question was whether he'd make it to the end of each night.

'How many rehearsals?'

'It would be best if we could do at least three nights in a row. Could that work?'

He sat back in his chair and took a deep breath. 'There's an old aircraft hangar near here. It's what we've used before for rehearsals.' He shook his head. 'The rest of the band are home for their holidays. I can't ask them to come back. But there's no reason we can't do the full rehearsal in the hangar.' He shrugged. 'I can play the guitar and sing as normal.' He gave her a little smile. 'There just won't be any screaming fans around us.'

She nodded slowly. 'What time do you normally do a gig?'

'Around nine o'clock at night. Why? Is it important?'

'Very. We need to do your rehearsal at the same time of day you'll actually be performing. On a performance day you'll burn up calories and carbohydrate at a different rate, at different times. After the performance we'll need to monitor your blood sugar late that night and the next morning. We don't want you to go home and hypo.'

He could feel a flicker of irritation. Why did things have to be so regimented? Sometimes after a gig he liked to party, sometimes he liked to chill out with the rest of the band and have a few beers. Sometimes his adrenaline was buzzing so hard it was hours before he could sleep. Would her strict inventory allow for that?

He sighed. Loudly. Frustration was just bubbling under the surface.

He was staring out of the window, watching as the garlands across the street flickered into a burst of colourful lights, one after the other.

He was conscious of her staring at him, running her fingers through her blonde curls and then lowering her head.

'You can be as mad as you like, Mitchell.' She'd started eating her chocolate cake again as if it was the most natural thing in the world. 'It doesn't change the fact that you're diabetic and I am your nurse.' She sipped at her rich coffee, smiling as it slid down her throat. 'You forget. I'm used to teenage tantrums.' She bit into a rich blob of cake and cream and raised her eyebrows. 'A rock-star temper tantrum is nothing to me.' A smile crept across her face as she shrugged. 'I can wait it out.'

She folded her arms across her chest and sat back in her chair.

He couldn't help the way the feelings of pleasure started to creep across his skin. Being in Sam's company was almost certainly becoming addictive. She could dissipate his frustration and anger in only a few words. No one else had ever been able to do that for him.

He grinned as she licked the last remnants of chocolate from the spoon. 'You're just trying to drive me crazy, aren't you?'

She raised her eyebrows suggestively as she took her last lick. 'I've no idea what you're talking about, Mitch.'

Sure she did. Because every time their flirtation went down that road she got that crazy little twinkle in her eye. If he could bottle and sell it, he could easily fund the hospital from now to eternity.

'You could have timed things a little better.'

She wrinkled her nose. 'What do you mean?'

He held out his arms. 'Look around you. We're in the middle of the festive season here. In three days' time it's Christmas Eve. Do you think I'll be able to book the hangar at nine o'clock on Christmas Eve? Who is going to want to work then?'

She shrugged. 'Who else do we need Mitch? Can't you flick an electrical switch to turn the power on? It's not like we have anything else to do.' As she said the words she looked up at him through lowered lids. 'It doesn't need to be anyone else but us.'

Oh, he could think of a whole host of other things to do. Rockets were currently firing through his veins. Mitchell Brody was known for being cool. But that was the last thing he was feeling right now.

He leaned over the table towards her, catching a waft of her perfume. 'You're right. It doesn't need to be anyone else but us.'

Her eyes locked with his. There it was. The unspoken implication. Made by both of them. He didn't have a single doubt they were on the same wavelength. There was no way he was reading this wrong.

He stood up and held out his hand towards her. 'Come on. We'll have a look around the rest of the shops before we head home.' She nodded and pushed her arms into her jacket. 'We won't have time tomorrow,' he added.

And there it was. Her sexy little smile appearing on her face once again. She put her hand in his. 'Sure, let's window-shop a little more.' She moved ahead of him, giving him his favourite view of her backside in figure-hugging jeans. She glanced over her shoulder at him as they approached the door. 'There are some things I just don't want to miss.'

CHAPTER TEN

Two nights. Two nights in a dark aircraft hangar with thudding music and ice cold air.

Only the air around them didn't seem that cold. The temperature between them was positively rising.

Watching Mitchell Brody thrash about the stage, singing his heart out, was igniting a whole new fire inside her.

There was something so primal about it. To all intents and purposes, when Mitch was on the stage he was as exposed as he'd ever be.

They'd fallen into an easy routine. He skied in the morning, they visited the hospital in the afternoon, had dinner together, then headed to rehearsals.

Only it wasn't so easy.

He'd hypoed a few times in the last two days, all because of the amount of energy he'd been expending. She'd reduced his insulin doses carefully, but each hypo had been another opportunity for amorous Mitchell to appear. They'd headed off the hypos quickly. He was recognising the symptoms as easily as she was. But the flirtations between them were making her internal temperature soar.

It all seemed to heading somewhere, she just wasn't quite sure where.

It had seemed like such a good idea at the time. Yesterday afternoon she'd felt bold. She'd felt flirtatious.

But the whole of today her stomach had been doing flip-flops.

Mitch was as cool as ever, cooking them a late breakfast then spending the time he always did down at the hospital. Christmas Eve in the hospital was magical. Even the sickest kids were excited.

Lisa was a blur, moving up and down the corridor at top speed. Mitch grabbed her arm on the way past. 'How's the list?'

She broke into a radiant smile and nodded her head. 'Come this way.'

She opened a door to a nearby cupboard. It was packed to the seams with brightly wrapped presents all with the children's names attached. 'The list is perfect. The delivery came right on schedule. With the amount of electronic gadgets you've just bought I think this place is going to spontaneously combust.' She was excited. It was clear—her eyes were sparkling and her hands never stopped moving.

'So, what's the plan? Same as last year?' He glanced towards Samantha.

'What did you do last year?'

Lisa laughed. 'Oh, Mitch doesn't only buy the presents. He likes to play Santa Claus too. He comes back at midnight, dresses up and puts the presents in each kid's room.'

'Really?' She couldn't believe it. Her brain was spinning. How far away was the hangar? Would he be able to rehearse and be back here on time? More importantly, would he be fit enough to do it?

'Do some of the kids wake up?'

Lisa nodded and gave a little sigh. 'Some of our kids are so sick that they're up most of the night. Catching sight of Santa Claus is a real boost for them.'

Mitch nodded. 'Except for last year, of course.' He exchanged a glance with Lisa.

Sam could tell from the expressions on their faces that they'd been caught. 'What happened?'

Lisa shook her head. 'Oh, genius here got caught by the three-year-old brother of one of our kids with leukaemia.'

Mitch rolled his eyes. 'Boy, did I. That little guy could talk for *hours*. He gave me a whole new list of toys that he wanted and Lisa and I were scrabbling about at three a.m., trying to find other presents for him.'

Samantha started laughing. 'And did you?'

Lisa nodded. 'Thankfully, we buy spares. We buy enough presents for the kids here, and their brothers and sisters. Some families spend their whole Christmas in hospital so we don't want anyone to miss out. We always think we've got things under control by having a list for every child. Then...we get Mr Three-in-the-Morning who wants things he's never mentioned before.'

Samantha was watching Mitch's face. 'Pressure was on then, Santa. The little guy met you in person. Can you imagine the bad press you would have got if you'd given him the wrong gifts?'

Mitch turned to Lisa. 'Is he here this year? Tell me if he is you'll sedate him with something.'

Lisa started laughing. 'No, Riley isn't here this year. His brother is currently in remission.'

Mitch's face broke into a wide smile. 'Oh, wow. That's great news.' It was just the way he said the words. The absolute genuineness in them. The way his shoulders sagged in pure relief. He was truly grateful that the little kid had turned a corner, because he knew how much that meant to the family.

Something curled up from deep inside her as she studied the small lines on his face around his eyes and mouth, and the intensity of his sincere brown eyes. As her eyes lowered to his mouth a little shiver shot up her spine, along with a sinking realisation.

Everything about Mitch Brody just cried out to her. From his masculine frustration at dealing with a new condition to his undivided devotion to this children's hospital and all its residents. This wasn't the guy she'd had a teenage crush on.

This was becoming a whole lot more.

Her breath caught in her throat. The thought panicked her. This was ridiculous. Okay, Mitchell Brody may have flirted with her, held her hand and kissed her. But there was no way he would even consider her in that way.

No, the woman Mitchell Brody would truly want would be a super-gorgeous, super-slim model or actress. She'd be a celebrity in her own right and they could be paid millions for their wedding pictures in some flash magazine.

Mitchell Brody wouldn't ever be interested in a girl like her. Why would he be, when he had so many other options?

She could feel tears prickling at the backs of her eyes. This was no one's fault but hers. She'd allowed herself to be drawn in by his sexy smile and charm. Who knew how many other women had had the same treatment from Mitch? This was probably just the norm for him, but her own sensibilities and emotions were reading things that probably weren't there. Maybe other women liked casual flings and flirtations, but that wasn't her. Being street smart wasn't really an aspect of her life. Oh, she could be street smart at work as a nurse, but as a regular human being?

'Sam, is something wrong?'

Lisa had walked back down the corridor and Mitch was standing right in front of her, his arms resting on her shoulders, his brown eyes studying her face. She blinked back the tears quickly. 'No. Of course not.' She shook her head, trying to convince herself as much as him.

He tilted his head to the side. He was still looking at her, obviously unconvinced by her answer. But thankfully he let it go, reaching down and taking her hand. 'Then let's go. We've got some planning to do, and it might be better if we chill out for an hour or so before we hit the rehearsals.' He spoke quietly. 'It's going to be a late night. I hope you're up for that on Christmas Eve.' The words were whispered in her ear, giving a sense of intimacy and sending electric pulses along her nerves.

This isn't what you imagine it to be. She tried to quell the thoughts running around her brain. This was about doing her job. This was about making Christmas special for these kids. This wasn't about her. It never would be.

'I'm fine with that,' she said quickly. 'It'll be nice to come back here later.' Her eyes swept up and down the corridor, taking in all the decorations and twinkling lights. The atmosphere around here was charged already. These kids, and their families, were *so* ready for Christmas. No matter what other crazy thoughts were going on in her head, she felt honoured to be a part of this.

It didn't matter that he was still holding her hand and the tingles were reaching up across her chest. She squeezed her eyes closed for a second as he led her down the corridor. But her attempt at a reality check did nothing for her body responses. They were all still completely tuned in to the radio station that was Mitchell Brody.

She let out a sigh. One more week. She could do this for one more week. Then she'd have enough money to pay her mum's nursing home fees for a whole year and she could get back to reality. Back to her school nursing job and her small flat that she'd always loved.

So, why all of a sudden, did it seem like not nearly enough?

Dave pulled the black SUV up outside the hangar. 'Wow, I knew it was an aircraft hangar, but I didn't expect it to be so—so big.'

Mitch smiled and he climbed out of the car and automatically reached for Sam's hand. He couldn't help himself.

Every time he was near her he just wanted to touch her—even if it was only for the briefest of seconds.

He opened the door to the hangar and switched on the electrical supply. The lights flickered, taking a few seconds to spring to life and show the true expanse around them. There was a stage at the other end, stretching from one side to the other.

Sam walked ahead, her freezing breath clearly visible in the air around them. She rubbed her arms up and down the sides of her bright blue jacket. 'Third night in a row and this place doesn't get any warmer. Brrr.'

He walked over and flung an arm around her shoulders. 'What did you expect? Balmy heating in the middle of the winter?'

She rested her head on his shoulder. 'Why do you have to practise somewhere so big?' Her voice was quiet, as if she was sad about something.

'Acoustics,' he said quickly. The place really was impersonal. And if he was honest, that really wasn't what he'd wanted for tonight. Things were changing between them—he wasn't sure how much longer he could keep his hands to himself.

He turned quickly and nodded to Dave, who was waiting at the door. 'Can you come back for us just after eleven and take us to the hospital?'

Dave gave a quick nod and wave and disappeared back outside the door. It only took a few seconds before they heard the engine of the SUV start up and he disappeared into the night.

Mitchell didn't hesitate. He crossed the hangar in long strides. He almost felt her bristle as he pulled away. But the temptation to pull her around into his arms and not concentrate on the job at hand was just too high.

This was it. This was the night he had to prove himself fit and well. If she gave a good report to the insurers the tour could go ahead with no problems. He'd worry about himself later. Right now, all he could let himself worry about was the kids in that hospital.

The air around him was practically dripping with ice. At a normal performance, by the time the band arrived, the sweat was in the air all around them. Temperatures in the venues usually went through the roof because of the number of bodies packed in tightly.

Would changing temperatures have any effect on his blood sugar? He had no idea.

He flung his jacket to the side and walked across the stage, grabbing his guitar and switching it on. The feedback in the open area let a loud squeal reverberate around the metal building.

Samantha looked so alone, standing in the middle of the concrete floor. The cold air made his skin prickle, but it wouldn't last long. As soon as he started playing and singing he would heat up.

He dug into the back pocket of his jeans and pulled out his monitor. He still hated it, but he had the routine of checking his blood-sugar level down to a fine art. The whole process could be completed in under twenty seconds. He'd done everything she'd suggested. Eaten a little more carbohydrate and reduced his insulin dose by a few units to see how much energy he used up during a performance. His big worry was not recognising signs of a hypo attack.

Tonight would be easier. This was his third rehearsal. He'd be looking for it every second. He wouldn't be distracted by the rest of the band and thousands of screaming fans. He wouldn't be carried away by the atmosphere and the electricity in the air.

Tonight was a solo performance for one.

On second thoughts, that might actually be worse.

He tucked the monitor back into his pocket and put his guitar strap over his shoulder, stepping up to the microphone. Rock music wasn't normally used as a serenade to women, but that's what it felt like right now.

He plucked the first notes on his guitar. It was time to get started.

Samantha was mesmerised. She couldn't help it.

After the first few minutes she forgot she was the only person in the room. For at least ten minutes it felt as if she was in a time warp. The kind you dreamed about as a teenager where your idol was singing only to you.

But this was no dream. This was reality. And no one could put a price on this.

The lights changed automatically with the music, going up and down depending on the tempo, and at certain points in the music sending strobes across the stage.

Mitchell was lost in the music, his body swaying as his fingers strummed out every tune and he belted out the lyrics into the microphone. He was singing as if there was a whole crowd in this room—not just her. He moved across the stage, rocking it out, jumping on speakers at high points in the songs and only slowing down when he sang the band's only rock ballad.

Every hair on her neck stood on edge, because at that point he was singing only to her.

Every time she closed her eyes she found herself swaying along to the music, murmuring the lyrics quietly.

After the first hour Mitchell stopped for a few seconds at the side of the stage. He picked up a container of milk and waved it at her, drinking most of it in under a minute. 'It's not the same as a beer,' he muttered into his microphone.

'Give it a few concerts,' she shouted back. 'When word gets out you'll be offered a million-pound contract to advertise milk!'

He looked up from the microphone. 'Will you drink it with me?' His gaze was heavy, his voice low, and even though the words echoed around the hangar it seemed like the most intimate, most loaded question in the world.

He didn't wait for an answer, just continued straight into his next set, strumming the guitar strings and moving on to the next song. 'Maybe,' she whispered under her breath. Could she really last another week around Mitch Brody?

'Sam? Sam, come up here.' His voice echoed around the hangar, yanking her out of her daydream. Her feet were frozen to the spot. Oh, no. This was the part that always made the headlines. The part where Mitch Brody pulled a fan from the crowd and serenaded her.

Except there wasn't a crowd here. There was only her. It was obvious Mitch was taking this rehearsal seriously. She shook her head. 'No, Mitch.'

'Yes, Sam.' She could see his smile reaching from ear to ear. He held out his hand towards her. It was so enticing. She could feel the pull—even from this far away. She could feel his warmth reaching out towards her across the frozen hangar.

Her feet started to move forward. She didn't want to go up on stage. That just wasn't her style and Mitch seemed to sense that, because as she neared the stage he started plucking at the strings of his guitar and singing one of the band's most popular slow songs. A million brides and grooms across the world must have danced to this.

But right now there was only him. And her.

Her throat was dry. She knew this was a performance, but it didn't feel like it. It felt like something much more personal. Something entirely for her.

He was reaching out to her again. The rock star under the spotlight. Every word was sending shivers down her spine and the blood racing around her body. Every tiny little hair was standing on end. All for her. Right up until the last note, the last string had been plucked and the last echo had faded around the hangar. Mesmerising.

Sweat was dripping from Mitch's hair, his face was flushed and skin glistening. She waited for a full minute before she walked over towards the front of the stage.

She was close enough to see his rapid breathing. Close enough to see his dilated pupils. Her brain switched into gear. Was this just the effects of the performance? Or was this the start of a hypo?

The selfish part of her wanted to think that she could have that effect on him. The professional part of her tried to be rational.

She bit her lip and stayed silent. It was important that Mitch recognise any symptoms himself. This had to form part of her assessment—whether she liked it or not.

What she really wanted to do was switch into nurse mode and go up and order him to test his blood sugar immediately. But that wasn't right for him, and that wasn't right for her.

So she waited.

After a few minutes he jumped down from the stage and walked over to her. His hair was tangled and damp, and she was sure she could practically smell the pheromones.

'What did you think?' His face was inches away from hers. All of a sudden he wasn't the distant teenage crush on stage, he was a living, breathing six-foot-four-inch man of sculpted muscle, sinfully dark eyes and perfect teeth right in front of her.

This was it. The final scene in the movie, when the hero swept the heroine into an embrace. She was holding her breath. Waiting for him to do something.

His head tilted to the side and his gaze narrowed. 'Didn't you like it?'

Her brain sprang back into life. 'I did. I-it was good. It was g-great,' she stammered.

'Great?' The look on his face was anything but. She'd said the wrong thing. Of course she had. He was an artist—

a performer. He revelled in his job and he wanted everyone to love it as much as he did.

There was a noise behind him as the door slammed open and a huge blast of icy wind swept around them.

'Ready, folks?' Dave shouted.

The disappointment in Mitch's eyes shone brighter than any spotlight. 'Yeah, we're ready,' he said, as he stalked back to the stage and picked up his leather jacket. 'Let's go.'

This time he walked straight past her towards the open door.

Her heart lurched in her chest. *It was spectacular. I loved it* echoed around her head. The words she'd been afraid to say out loud. Afraid she would reveal exactly how she felt around him. This was so much harder than she'd anticipated. So much harder than she'd expected. Being a fan and admiring someone from afar was *so* different from admitting to yourself that you felt so much more. And it was so much harder when you knew there was no point.

She sighed and turned around. Next year she'd think twice. If she couldn't work with Daniel's family—the little boy with CF—then she'd have to reassess her finances. Maybe it was time to change jobs again? She had to think of a way to stop being so financially dependent on this extra work.

Not when this was the price.

Mitchell felt as if a black fog was hanging around his head. Was his ego really that big? Just because Samantha hadn't fawned over his performance?

The snow-covered roads were passing swiftly outside. He needed to pull himself out of this mire. Christmas Eve was usually his favourite time of year. Sneaking around the hospital and putting the presents out for the kids was always special. There was always some pale-faced little person who was awake and wanted to open their present in front of Santa. He couldn't hide the joy that gave him. Seeing the little eyes widen at the gift of their dreams and knowing that he'd given just a little happiness to a child who might not have a lot of time left on this earth.

The thoughts strengthened his resolve. He couldn't let anything get in the way of this. He would do anything to make sure he continued to provide for these kids.

Anything at all.

The car pulled up to a halt outside the hospital. It was eleven-thirty. Hardly time to get ready at all. Thankfully Lisa was waiting, the costume, beard, shoes and Santa sack already laid out. She put her fingers to her lips and led them into the staff changing room. 'Shhh, we have a few still awake. And it looks like you're going to have to come back and refill your sack at least five times. I've put the presents in for the kids in Rooms 4, 5 and 6 first. They are furthest away.'

Mitch nodded and stripped off his clothes without a second thought. 'Give me five minutes, Lisa. I need to shower.'

She slipped out of the room into the darkened corridor, leaving Sam and him alone. The silence was deafening. He took out his monitor and spent twenty seconds checking his level. It was on the way down so he'd need to eat something soon, but it wasn't urgent.

Sam was bent over the Christmas parcels, organising the next load for the sack. He flicked the switch on the shower, filling the room with steam.

It was almost as if she was waiting to say something to him. Trying to work things out in her head. But Mitch wasn't feeling rational—he wasn't feeling patient. For some reason the pent-up frustration and anger from earlier was returning. He had a million fans around the world. Why did the opinion of Samantha Lewis, his nurse, matter so much? Three weeks ago he hadn't even known her. He would have walked past her in the street without a second glance.

Well, maybe that wasn't quite true. There was no way he wouldn't have noticed those big blue eyes and jeans-covered curves.

He just couldn't work out why what she thought mattered so much. This wasn't about the diabetes any more. Granted, he still wanted her to give her blessing for the tour. But how she looked at him, what she said to him, how she felt about him seemed to matter so much more.

She was still hovering around. So he did what any self-respecting guy would. He dropped his boxers on the floor and stepped into the shower, giving her a view of his naked backside.

Some girls would have paid money for that. Samantha Lewis wouldn't.

Mitch had never been shy about his body. After a few weeks of looking a little puny, his muscle tone and weight was starting to return. In another few weeks—just in time to start the tour—he should look normal again.

He heard her choke a little outside. Was it the steam? Or was it something else?

When he emerged from the shower a few minutes later she'd made a sharp exit into the corridor. He was disappointed. But what had he expected to happen here, in a staff changing room?

He pulled on the costume, fixed the beard to his face and lifted the sack. It was like a rush of pure endorphins. Playing Santa for these kids was the best job in the world.

Sam was waiting at the door, shifting on her feet continuously. 'Do you want me to sit down somewhere and wait for you?'

Of course. Part of him wanted to say yes. He loved doing this. But the reluctance he thought he might feel wasn't there. He kind of wanted Sam to play a part in this too. He was sure she would find it every bit as magical as he did.

He shook his head and gestured for her to follow him

along the corridor. It was dark, lit only by the multicoloured lights and white stars that were wound around the windows and strung across the ceiling.

The bells that were stitched into the sleeves of his coat jangled gently as he moved down the corridor. Sam let out a nervous laugh. 'I love it,' she whispered. 'It's almost as if they can hear the reindeers and sleigh landing on the roof.'

He raised his eyebrows. 'Watch out. There's a thought. I should have made you dress up as a reindeer.'

The nerves and anxiety previously obvious on her face were gone. Now all he could see was the softness of her eyes. The jingling continued as he reached the first room. Lukas Wagner was fast asleep. He was recovering from emergency cardiac valve surgery and his colour had improved rapidly in the last few days. Mitchell moved quietly, slotting the gift-wrapped tablet and games machine into the carefully positioned stocking at the bottom of the bed. Sam added various little extras from the bag she carried, mainly nuts, fruit and chocolate, and they both crept back out.

Anna Gruber, in the next room, was also sleeping. She'd wished for a pink tablet and crying baby doll. Her sleepy mother gave them both a wave from where she was dozing in the recliner chair, whispering her thanks as they left.

It was Brian Flannigan's room next. The teenager had made some progress towards recovering from his recent dip in health. His wasn't a small electronic parcel. His was a full-scale guitar. Sam smiled as Mitchell pulled it from the sack and ran his fingers over the gold paper.

'Do you think the wrapping is a bit of a giveaway?'

He smiled. 'You try wrapping one of these things. It's no easy task.' He pushed open the door and Brian's eyes flickered open immediately.

He blinked again, taking a few seconds to recognise the thinly disguised Santa Claus. 'Mitch,' he croaked, as he tried to push himself up in the bed.

'Hey, buddy.' It was so nice to see him with a little more colour about his face. He was still thin and pale, but he was obviously managing to eat a little better.

'Am I supposed to pretend to be sleeping when Santa Claus appears?'

Mitch sat down next to the bed. 'You can do whatever you like. I'm just glad to see you're looking better and that you're out of isolation for a while.'

Brian nodded. 'I've responded well to the antibodies they've given me. But I'm still on the bone-marrow transplant list.' He didn't sound nearly as breathless as he had before. He gave a weak smile. 'They told me today that there's a possible match. In the next few days I could be a new guy.' There was such hope in his voice—the possibility of an end to all this sickness—that Mitch wanted to reach over and hug him, but instead he squeezed his hand. 'That's the best news you could give me.'

Brian nodded towards the present. 'Santa's brought me a guitar.' He glanced around the room. 'Is it midnight yet? Can I open it?'

'Absolutely.' He was trying not to let tears form in his eyes. He knew what this little guy had ahead. A bone-marrow transplant could be the gift of life, just like it had been for his brother. If the match was confirmed, sample collected and things went well, Brian Flannigan could be walking out of here to a whole new way of life.

Testing for the next few years would be inevitable. But after that? No more avoiding every single friend with a sniffle or sore stomach. No more worrying about sports and activities he couldn't take part in. Mitchell couldn't help but smile and say a silent prayer that Brian would be as lucky as his brother had been.

Brian ripped at the gold paper, tearing it off in a few quick strips. His eyes grew as wide as saucers. 'Oh wow!

A Fender.' He hugged the black guitar towards his chest. 'It's the best thing I've ever seen. Is it mine? Really?'

Mitch nodded. 'Really. Once this bone-marrow transplant is done, I expect to hear that you're practising all the time.'

For the first time in a long time Brian's cheeks actually looked flushed. 'Oh, I will. I promise. This is the best Christmas *ever*!'

Mitch stood up, giving him a tap on the shoulder. 'I'll see you some time in the next few days, buddy. Meanwhile, Santa has other presents to deliver.'

As he left the room Brian was already starting to strum the guitar strings as he lay in bed. Samantha was waiting by the door, the expression on her face matching entirely how he felt. She placed her hand over her chest. 'Oh, Mitch, I thought I was going to cry. That's such great news for him. I hope it works out.'

'So do I.' He'd whispered the words. A whole host of memories was flooding around him, reinforcing just how important all this was.

Sam walked over and laid her hands on his chest. 'I get why you do this, Mitch. I really do. I just wish the world could know you like I do.' She wound her hands around his neck and stood up on tiptoe.

He responded immediately, his whole body in tune with hers. Nothing and no one could get between them now. Their lips made contact, hers soft and sweet with a taste of warm orange. The girl had more lip balms than he had guitars. His hands went automatically to her hips, pulling her towards him. Everything about this felt so right. She was the girl who was meant to fill his arms. He'd never felt this way about anyone before. No one else had ever come close.

This wasn't meaningless press-associated passion. This was heartfelt and true. And the more he kissed her, the more he resented the barriers in his way—they were in a corridor in the children's hospital, and all items of clothing had to stay exactly where they were. Imagine the scandal if a partially dressed Santa Claus was found in a compromising position!

No. It was the other kind of barriers. The emotional ones that made him feel as if he'd had to build a fortress about himself. His diabetes. His tour. His responsibilities. And the ugly, black fact that he'd been quite willing to try and charm her, to manipulate her to keep his tour on track.

He didn't want her to go. The thought of Sam getting on a plane to go home when her contract was up made him want to pull her even closer. He didn't want to let her go.

His natural instincts were to deepen the kiss, to slide his hands underneath her short jumper and feel the softness of her skin. But even he knew that was for later—not here, and not now.

Instead, he pulled back gently, a smile reaching from ear to ear. 'What do you say we deliver these presents as quickly as possible?' His sleeve tinkled as he moved it. 'My reindeer are getting impatient on the roof.'

She blinked, her pupils wide in the dim lights, and smiled back at him. 'I think this could be a busy night for Santa, he'd better not waste any time.'

And he didn't. He refilled his sack four times as he supplied presents to every room, pausing only to speak to a little girl, Anneline, who wanted to know if he could bring his reindeer into her room. She was more than happy when he suggested she open one of her presents instead, and wrapped her arms around a blonde-haired doll as she went back to sleep.

Mitchell's legs were working nearly as quickly as his brain. No time for Santa-suit removal. He grabbed Samantha's hand once he'd delivered the last present, tossed the Santa sack and beard back in the staffroom and grabbed their jackets. 'Let's go.'

The car was outside, waiting for them. Dave had already been sent home and Mitch let her take the lead. She jumped in, and he drove the car back up the mountain towards his house.

The air in the car was thick was tension. Instead of laughing and joking, neither one of them said a word, willing the miles to speed past on the dark road. It was late but he didn't feel tired. It would probably be best to have something to eat when he reached the house, but if Sam had other priorities...how could he argue?

The car finally skidded to a halt outside the house and both them were out of the car in a matter of seconds. The only lights on in the house were the twinkling red and gold ones lighting up the Christmas tree and the sparkling gold stars strung along the walls. Could there be a more perfect setting?

He slammed the door behind him with one hand and reached for Sam with the other, pressing her against the wall. Her leg hitched against his hip and her arms wound around his neck. 'Where were we?' he murmured, as he unzipped her padded blue jacket and threw it to the floor.

Her lips touched his neck. 'I think we were right about here,' she whispered, as the brush of her skin against his sent his senses alight. He shrugged off his leather jacket, quickly followed by the top half of the Santa costume. Now was the time to get rid of layers—the quicker the better.

He moved her around, keeping her in his arms and walking her backwards towards the sofa. One arm twitched. Just a little, but enough to distract him from the overwhelming surge of hormones. He kept walking, pushing her gently onto the sofa and positioning himself above her.

There it was again. Just as he moved his hand to redistribute his weight, a little tremor. He paused above her neck. Her eyes were half-closed, her lips just begging him to touch them. His body was reacting just the way it should—and just the way it shouldn't.

He tried to ignore it. Tried to ignore the nagging voices in his head. But it was the oddest feeling. Almost fight or flight. Survival instinct. He pulled back, changing his position from lying above her to sitting on the sofa by her feet.

'Mitch? What's wrong?'

He wanted to scream in frustration. He'd known earlier that his blood-sugar level had been on its way down. He should have found something to eat then.

She sat upright, tugging at her displaced jumper, obviously wondering what on earth she'd done wrong. He pushed himself to his feet, shifting his trousers to a more accommodating position and heading for the kitchen. 'I'm sorry. Give me five minutes.'

Was this it? Was this how things were going to be for the rest of his life? Was his sex life going to be ruled by his blood-sugar levels? His fingers tightened into a fist, his nails burning into the palms of his hands.

He yanked open the nearest cupboard door, grabbed a couple of chocolate biscuits and ate quickly. He could feel sweat breaking out on his body and the tremble of his hands was getting worse. The rest of the biscuits were slammed off the nearest wall.

His monitor was in the back pocket of his jeans. With growing frustration he sat down at the table and started to go through the motions. He waited for the beep and, sure enough, his blood-sugar level was low. Lower than when he'd checked earlier, but not as low as when they'd deliberately made him hypo.

He ran his fingers through his hair. He could feel his heart thudding in his chest. How long would this take? How long until he started to feel the effects of the chocolate getting into his bloodstream?

There was a movement out of the corner of his eye. Sam.

Standing in the doorway with her hands folded across her chest. He couldn't read the expression on her face. Couldn't read it at all.

Eventually she walked over and sat down next to him, spinning his monitor round and pressing the button to see the last result.

'Why didn't you tell me, Mitch?' Her voice was quiet, but she was closer now, and it was clear from the look in her eyes that she felt hurt.

He felt a wave of panic. His mouth started to run away with him. 'I should have eaten earlier—but I felt fine. I checked my level and meant to eat before we left the hospital. You told me I had to be able to recognise the signs of a hypo and act myself. Well, that's what I did. Even though I wanted to be doing something else entirely.' He couldn't help the implication in his voice.

He could see her suck in a deep breath. 'What have you eaten?'

'Biscuits. I've had two biscuits. I'll be fine in a minute. Just give me a minute. Don't judge me on this. You can't do anything that will affect the tour. I'll be fine on tour. This was our first real practice. I'll know now to eat when I come off stage, whether I want to or not.'

He started to shake his head. 'This tour is far too important. Far too important to let this diabetes get in the way of. Don't say anything about this, Sam. You won't, will you? Because I recognised the signs. I did what I was supposed to do.'

She moved her hand across the table as if she were about to touch him, then pulled it back. '*You're* too important, Mitch. Not the tour. I get that you recognised the signs. But I still think it's too early. I still think there's a danger you might be distracted by other things and not recognise the signs in time. Tonight it was only you and me. What happens when it's twenty thousand fans shouting for an encore? What will you do then?'

He shrugged. 'I'll eat something and play it.'

'It's not that simple, Mitch. You know it isn't.' She stood up. 'This is my fault. I've crossed a line with you that I shouldn't have. I'm supposed to be your nurse. I'm supposed to be looking after you—not kissing you!' She flung her arms up in frustration and started shaking her head.

'I can't do this any more, Mitch. This isn't working. And I definitely have reservations about saying you're fit for a tour that starts in ten days.'

'What? You've got to be joking.' Now the panic was truly setting in. 'You've *got* to say I'm fit for this tour. Everything depends on it. Those kids depend on it. If I don't do this tour, they don't get their new hospital. I don't care what happens to me, I care about what happens to them. No one else can fund the place the way I can. I *need* this money. I *need* this tour.'

He started to pace. Irrational thoughts were spinning around his head. What did she mean—she couldn't do this any more? Surely she didn't mean him and her? Because that was the one thing that was right in all this.

Her face was pale and her eyes wide. 'What are you talking about? St Jude's? The money is for the hospital? That's why you're so desperate to do this tour?'

She started shaking her head again. 'Why on earth wouldn't you tell me? Is that why you can't rearrange the tour? You wouldn't be able to give them money?' She frowned. 'How much money are we talking about here?'

But he wasn't listening. He was focusing on her frown and shaking head. All he could think about was that she might actually say no. More importantly, he couldn't stop his obvious hesitation.

'I wasn't sure. I didn't know if I could trust you. I don't

tell anyone about the hospital. *Anyone*. The press would have a field day if they knew I was involved.'

Her eyes were wide with disbelief. 'You're paying to re-build the whole hospital? Can't they get money from some-where else?'

He shook his head. 'They've tried, time and time again. I can't let this place disappear. This place was the differ-ence between my brother living and dying. The difference between my family unravelling at the seams and staying strong and happy.'

'So why didn't you just say?' She was shouting now, ob-viously exasperated by all this. 'You don't trust me? What have I ever done, or said, that made you think you couldn't trust me? Why would I tell anyone about this?'

He ran his fingers through his hair. It was like a perma-nent fog had settled around his brain. 'It isn't you, Sam. But I've been down this road before. I've been sold out by a friend. I couldn't take the risk. Not with St Jude's. It's just too important. Too special.'

'And I'm not?' The words hung in the air between them. He was so confused. All he could think about was trying to protect the hospital.

'What will it take, Samantha? How much? Just tell me and I'll give it to you. I know you need money for your mum's nursing-home care—how much do you need?'

Her head shot up. 'What?' The frown deepened, accom-panied by a look of fury as she stepped right up to him with her hands on her hips. *'What?'*

Where had those words come from? His brain was still in that slight hypo state. The one where there were no safe-guards, no reservations on what he said. He felt as if he were a few seconds behind everything. What had she just said? *And I'm not?*

'You're trying to buy me off? You honestly think I would do something like that?'

She didn't hesitate for a second, just spun on her heel and grabbed for her bag. As she walked past she swept her jacket from the floor.

'Sam...' He was still panicking. Now for a whole host of other reasons. She was special. More special than anyone he'd ever met. He just hadn't had a chance to tell her yet. And as soon as this fog lifted from his head, he would.

She turned back and marched up to his face, putting her finger inches from his nose. 'Don't you dare. Don't you dare say another word. I'll send an email. I'll let you do your damn tour. But I'll recommend you have another diabetic nurse with you every step of the way. If they're happy to take that risk, that's up to them. But don't you dare put this on me.'

She grabbed the car keys from the table and stamped across the room, leaving the door wide open and an icy blast circulating around him.

His focus was starting to return. The sugar burst was finally making him come to his senses. Oh, no. What had he done?

He stood up, his legs still a little shaky, and walked to the door.

But it was too late. Tyres squealed as she disappeared into the night.

She couldn't think straight. She was so angry. It was her own fault—his too. But she'd been delusional to think there was ever a chance of anything happening between them when the guy obviously didn't trust her.

The tears started rolling down her cheeks. What on earth was she going to do? It was after midnight on Christmas Eve. She was in Austria. She didn't have any friends here. There wasn't exactly anywhere else for her to go.

The road signs loomed before her. Airport. Yes. Where else could she go? There would still be flights, and the one thing she was sure of was that she had her passport in her bag.

She turned the wheel and put her foot on the accelerator. It was time to get away from here. It was time to get away from Mitchell Brody.

It was time to get on with her life.

CHAPTER ELEVEN

'THIS HAD BETTER be good, Mitch, it's three o'clock on Christmas morning.' Mitch bristled at Dave's words. He hated having to do this.

'I need a lift. In fact, I just need the car.'

'You've got a car.'

'I don't. Samantha took it when she left.'

'She left? Where has she gone?'

'I don't know.' He sagged against the wall and listened to the monster-size groan at the end of the phone.

'You idiot. What have you done? She was the best thing that's happened to you in years.'

He tried to swallow the huge lump in his throat. Dave was one of the only people on this planet who would speak to him like this. But it was exactly what he needed. 'I know.' He struggled to get the words out. A thought flickered into his brain. 'She hasn't appeared at your place, has she?'

'Not yet she hasn't. And I doubt she would. If you've upset her I'm probably the last person she wants to see.'

'But where on earth could she be?' He was sounding desperate and he knew it. 'She liked the skating rink— maybe there? Or the Christmas tree in the square?'

'Are you nuts? Have you any idea what the temperature is out there? This is the worst night of the year to try and find somewhere to go. Everywhere is closed for Christmas.'

He squeezed his eyes closed. 'You're right.' Worry was beginning to wash over him. She was out there. Alone. And it was his fault.

'Where would you go in a foreign country after a fight with a fool of a man?' Dave clearly wasn't going to forgive him for this. 'Did she take anything with her?'

'Just her bag.'

'So she has the car and her handbag, which might contain her passport?'

His eyes opened. 'Do you think she's headed to the airport? But she doesn't have her suitcase, she doesn't have her clothes.'

Dave sighed. 'I think we can safely assume she's not caring about any of that right now. Give me ten minutes. I'll pick you up. And, Mitch?'

'Yeah?'

'We're not done talking about this.' He hung up the phone.

Mitch almost smiled. Dave was going to blast him all the way to the airport and back. But he didn't care. He just hoped she was there. He just hoped she was safe.

His eyes fell on the little blue-wrapped box next to the phone. The present he'd bought her. The one he'd spent nearly an hour deliberating over. He'd wanted to give it to her tonight once they were back from St Jude's, but he'd forgotten all about it.

He turned the little box over in his hands.

Would she like it?

Would she talk to him again? Would she even agree to *see* him again?

He had no idea.

But one thing was crystal-clear.

He was willing to spend the rest of his life trying to find out.

* * *

The short-stay car park was the most expensive at the airport. But Samantha was determined not to think about it. Once she was back in the UK, she'd phone Dave and let him know where to pick up the car.

She hurried across the concourse in the airport, her footsteps echoing all around her. The place was virtually deserted with only minimal staff in place. There was a tired-faced woman behind the desk of the most popular UK airline. 'Do you have any flights back to the UK?'

The woman nodded and smiled wearily. 'There's one taking off at six a.m.' She glanced at the clock. 'You can buy a ticket for the next fifteen minutes. After that, there isn't another flight until five p.m.'

'I'll take it.' She pulled her passport and credit card from her bag, trying not to recoil visibly as the woman said the price out loud.

It only took a few minutes to process the payment and print out her paperwork. Samantha smiled thankfully and turned to look across the airport.

It was almost as if all her energy suddenly started to leave her body. She'd been running on pure adrenaline, and there just wasn't any left. Her shoulders sagged and her legs started to shake. She walked to the nearest seat and sat down for a few minutes, trying to pull herself together.

It was easier to lean forward, her head almost between her knees. But she couldn't get comfortable, the thick, bright blue jacket limiting her movements. In a last spurt of frustration she tugged the jacket off. The airport was warm so there was no need for it in there, and even though she'd loved the jacket, it was another reminder of Mitch. She emptied the pockets and stuffed it in the trash can next to her.

It would be cold when she got back to the UK, but she'd

worry about it then. For now she didn't need anything else to remind her of how much she'd screwed up here.

She didn't want to wear something that he'd bought her. The very fact that she'd allowed him to buy her anything now stung like a scorpion. If she could possibly have refused her salary for the last few weeks, she would have. But any day now she'd need to make another payment to her mother's nursing home. This wasn't just about her. Like Mitchell, she had responsibilities.

That thought made her breath catch in her throat. His financial responsibilities were every bit as important to him as hers were to her. She could understand that, she could. There was nothing she wouldn't do in order to keep her mother in the best place possible.

'You really don't want the jacket?'

The bland words sent a shard through her heart. She couldn't help but sit bolt upright. She was almost afraid to turn around, afraid of where the next steps would take her. Because the last few had been difficult enough.

But she didn't need to. Mitchell walked around in front of her, kneeling down until their faces were on a level. He tugged at the sleeve of the jacket still sticking out of the trash can. 'It's a pity, you know, it really is your colour.'

'I don't want it to be.'

'But haven't you noticed? Sometimes things are just naturally matched together, even when you fight against it? And even when you don't completely understand why?'

He wasn't talking about a jacket any more.

It was just him and her. He was looking at her with those deep brown eyes. There was no sexy, charming smile. There was no cheeky twinkle. All she could see was complete sincerity.

She squeezed her eyes shut, willing the tears that had automatically formed not to spill down her cheeks. It was easier not to look at him. 'You didn't trust me, Mitchell.

You thought I might sell you out for money. You thought I would betray the staff and those kids at the hospital for money.' She pressed her hand to her chest and this time she did open her eyes. 'That's the kind of person you believe me to be.'

He shook his head fiercely. 'No. No, I don't. I'm just so used to protecting that place, so used to counting on one hand the number of people that I can actually trust, that I was on autopilot.'

'You were on autopilot?' She couldn't hide the scorn in her voice. 'And did that apply to everything we did together—autopilot?'

He didn't hesitate in his response. 'Absolutely not. Definitely not.' He reached out to touch her but she pulled her hand away as if he'd given her an electric shock.

She couldn't deal with the sensation of how her body reacted to his on top of everything else.

'Can't you tell that everything between us was special—was meant to be?' This time he didn't let her shy away. His hand reached out and cupped her cheek.

'I didn't know that this diabetes would be the best thing that could happen to me. I didn't know that it would bring me you.'

Her heart was thudding in her chest. She wanted to believe all this, she wanted to respond. But too many other things were getting in the way. What if this was all just an elaborate plan to continue with the tour?

She shook her head. She couldn't meet his eyes. She didn't want to be sucked in by the pleading look in his deep eyes.

'You can't play me, Mitch. I won't be part of your façade. I've told you. I'll send the email saying you can do the tour—as long as you have supervision. And I don't care who that is, as long as it's not me.' She waved her hands. 'I can bet there will be a million specialist nurses who can't wait to help you out. I can even give you a recommendation or two.'

'Is that what it will take?'

The short answer pulled her back into the present. 'What do you mean?'

He stood up, grabbing her arms and pulling her towards him, his face inches from hers. She didn't even have the opportunity to move as he put a hand on either hip and held her firmly in place.

'Is that what it will take? Hiring someone else to be my nurse, to get you to come back? Because I'll do it. I'll do anything you want. I would much rather that *you* were my nurse.' He tilted his head to the side. 'You have a certain way with you.'

She couldn't focus. 'Why, why would you want me to come back?'

He shifted his hand from her hip and pressed it on her chest. 'Because I can't think without you. I can't sleep without you. I can't breathe without you. And none of it is to do with a medical condition. I need you, Samantha. There is no me without you.'

'You can't mean that.'

'I can. I know how I feel. I want that moment back, Sam. That moment in the hangar when it was just you and me. You were looking up at me on the stage as if I were the only man in the world. I want that. I want that for a lifetime.' He moved his hand to his chest. 'I know how I feel in here. Tell me you don't feel that way too. Tell me right now, and I'll let you get on that plane back to England. I'll pay your fees and never see you again.' His voice was getting desperate as his emotions were overcoming him.

She felt her legs start to tremble again. The one thing she didn't want. The one thing she could never want. Never to see Mitchell Brody again. Never hear his voice, never feel the touch of his skin next to hers. It was almost unbearable.

A tear rolled down her cheek. 'I don't know, Mitch. I just don't know.' She was shaking her head again. 'I'm so angry at you for not trusting me. I don't know how to get past that.'

He nodded. 'I know. It's like my brain doesn't function properly when I'm having a hypo. It feels as if all bets are off. My mouth says all the things that ever flit through my brain—even just for a second. You know, the thousands of things that you would never actually say out loud. I can't control it, Sam. I really can't.' He reached up and stroked her hair. 'Just know that it's not how I really feel. It's not what I really think. I love you, Sam. I don't want you to go anywhere. In fact, whatever you want, just name it. I'll do anything for you, Sam Lewis.'

She bit her lip. She had experienced this before. She had seen the quietest kids in the world have a hypoglycaemic attack and become completely unrecognisable—say and do things she would never have expected. Mitch wasn't so unusual. He'd been desperate. He was trying to save the place that had helped give him his brother back.

He reached into his pocket. 'If you'd waited another five minutes, my head would have been back in place and I could have told you all this then. I also could have given you this.' He held out the little blue box.

'What is it?' Her hands were trembling as she pulled at the little ribbon on top of the box. She lifted the lid. There, sitting on the pale blue velvet, was a thick silver bracelet and beautiful silver charm in the shape of a pair of skates. Along the blades glittered clear white stones—she could only guess they were diamonds.

It was the charm she'd spotted in the window of the shop in Innsbruck. Only the charm had been customised. Another few bright blue stones glittered next to the catch on the bracelet. It was truly beautiful.

She was struck by how thoughtful the gift was. Mitchell Brody was wealthy enough to buy the biggest diamond necklace or ring in the world. But it would be meaningless to her.

This wasn't. This was something that they'd shared together. Something he'd valued enough to make special for her.

He pointed to the blue stones. 'They match your eyes. Just the perfect colour.'

She smiled. 'It's beautiful, Mitch. I love it. Thank you.'

He looked scared to smile in return. 'What does that mean? What does that mean for us? Will you stay?'

She shook her head and spoke quietly. 'I'm not going to stay, Mitch.' She wound her hands around his neck. 'I'm going to go home to see my mum.'

His face fell. She'd never seen him look so wounded, so dejected. So she pressed her lips close to his ear. 'But I'm kind of hoping you'll come with me. I'm hoping you'll decide to spend the few days between now and your tour coming home with me to meet my mum.' She laughed. 'I can't possibly consider dating someone my mum hasn't met yet.' She got serious again. 'I want that moment back too, Mitch. You and me. For a lifetime. I want to hear you sing like that to me every night for the rest of my life.'

She could feel the tension dissipate throughout his body, the relief flood through his veins. He turned his face to press his lips next to hers. 'I think I can do that.' He slid his hands down her sides. 'And dating? Is that what we're going to be doing? Because I'm versatile with my singing,' he whispered in her ear. 'I can even do it naked.'

She raised herself up on tiptoe. 'Well, we've got to start somewhere,' she said with a twinkle in her eye, 'but let me keep that naked singing as a definite possibility.' And she kissed him, over and over again.

EPILOGUE

PRESS RELEASE:

After disappearing for a few months after his spectacular worldwide tour Mitchell Brody seems to have been making good use of his time.

He's just announced that he's married twenty-nine-year-old Samantha Lewis, who was originally acting as his nurse after his surprise diagnosis with diabetes last year. Mitchell, who is now an ambassador for diabetes worldwide, also announced the arrival of his son, Jude Shaun Brody, who was born last night weighing seven pounds three ounces.

He and his family ask for some privacy at this time to enjoy married life and their new arrival.

* * * * *

Mills & Boon® Hardback

November 2014

ROMANCE

A Virgin for His Prize	Lucy Monroe
The Valquez Seduction	Melanie Milburne
Protecting the Desert Princess	Carol Marinelli
One Night with Morelli	Kim Lawrence
To Defy a Sheikh	Maisey Yates
The Russian's Acquisition	Dani Collins
The True King of Dahaar	Tara Pammi
Rebel's Bargain	Annie West
The Million-Dollar Question	Kimberly Lang
Enemies with Benefits	Louisa George
Man vs. Socialite	Charlotte Phillips
Fired by Her Fling	Christy McKellen
The Twelve Dates of Christmas	Susan Meier
At the Chateau for Christmas	Rebecca Winters
A Very Special Holiday Gift	Barbara Hannay
A New Year Marriage Proposal	Kate Hardy
A Little Christmas Magic	Alison Roberts
Christmas with the Maverick Millionaire	Scarlet Wilson

MEDICAL

Playing the Playboy's Sweetheart	Carol Marinelli
Unwrapping Her Italian Doc	Carol Marinelli
A Doctor by Day...	Emily Forbes
Tamed by the Renegade	Emily Forbes

Mills & Boon® Large Print

November 2014

ROMANCE

Christakis's Rebellious Wife	Lynne Graham
At No Man's Command	Melanie Milburne
Carrying the Sheikh's Heir	Lynn Raye Harris
Bound by the Italian's Contract	Janette Kenny
Dante's Unexpected Legacy	Catherine George
A Deal with Demakis	Tara Pammi
The Ultimate Playboy	Maya Blake
Her Irresistible Protector	Michelle Douglas
The Maverick Millionaire	Alison Roberts
The Return of the Rebel	Jennifer Faye
The Tycoon and the Wedding Planner	Kandy Shepherd

HISTORICAL

A Lady of Notoriety	Diane Gaston
The Scarlet Gown	Sarah Mallory
Safe in the Earl's Arms	Liz Tyner
Betrayed, Betrothed and Bedded	Juliet Landon
Castle of the Wolf	Margaret Moore

MEDICAL

200 Harley Street: The Proud Italian	Alison Roberts
200 Harley Street: American Surgeon in London	Lynne Marshall
A Mother's Secret	Scarlet Wilson
Return of Dr Maguire	Judy Campbell
Saving His Little Miracle	Jennifer Taylor
Heatherdale's Shy Nurse	Abigail Gordon

Mills & Boon® Hardback

December 2014

ROMANCE

Taken Over by the Billionaire	Miranda Lee
Christmas in Da Conti's Bed	Sharon Kendrick
His for Revenge	Caitlin Crews
A Rule Worth Breaking	Maggie Cox
What The Greek Wants Most	Maya Blake
The Magnate's Manifesto	Jennifer Hayward
To Claim His Heir by Christmas	Victoria Parker
Heiress's Defiance	Lynn Raye Harris
Nine Month Countdown	Leah Ashton
Bridesmaid with Attitude	Christy McKellen
An Offer She Can't Refuse	Shoma Narayanan
Breaking the Boss's Rules	Nina Milne
Snowbound Surprise for the Billionaire	Michelle Douglas
Christmas Where They Belong	Marion Lennox
Meet Me Under the Mistletoe	Cara Colter
A Diamond in Her Stocking	Kandy Shepherd
Falling for Dr December	Susanne Hampton
Snowbound with the Surgeon	Annie Claydon

MEDICAL

Midwife's Christmas Proposal	Fiona McArthur
Midwife's Mistletoe Baby	Fiona McArthur
A Baby on Her Christmas List	Louisa George
A Family This Christmas	Sue MacKay

Mills & Boon® Large Print
December 2014

ROMANCE

Zarif's Convenient Queen	Lynne Graham
Uncovering Her Nine Month Secret	Jennie Lucas
His Forbidden Diamond	Susan Stephens
Undone by the Sultan's Touch	Caitlin Crews
The Argentinian's Demand	Cathy Williams
Taming the Notorious Sicilian	Michelle Smart
The Ultimate Seduction	Dani Collins
The Rebel and the Heiress	Michelle Douglas
Not Just a Convenient Marriage	Lucy Gordon
A Groom Worth Waiting For	Sophie Pembroke
Crown Prince, Pregnant Bride	Kate Hardy

HISTORICAL

Beguiled by Her Betrayer	Louise Allen
The Rake's Ruined Lady	Mary Brendan
The Viscount's Frozen Heart	Elizabeth Beacon
Mary and the Marquis	Janice Preston
Templar Knight, Forbidden Bride	Lynna Banning

MEDICAL

200 Harley Street: The Soldier Prince	Kate Hardy
200 Harley Street: The Enigmatic Surgeon	Annie Claydon
A Father for Her Baby	Sue MacKay
The Midwife's Son	Sue MacKay
Back in Her Husband's Arms	Susanne Hampton
Wedding at Sunday Creek	Leah Martyn